SERVANT MAGE

ALSO BY KATE ELLIOTT

Unconquerable Sun

Black Wolves

The Golden Key
(with Melanie Rawn and
Jennifer Roberson)

The Labyrinth Gate

The Very Best of Kate Elliott
(collection)

**THE COURT OF FIVES
TRILOGY**

Court of Fives

Poisoned Blade

Buried Heart

**THE SPIRITWALKER
TRILOGY**

Cold Magic

Cold Fire

Cold Steel

**THE CROSSROADS
TRILOGY**

Spirit Gate

Shadow Gate

Traitors' Gate

**THE CROWN OF STARS
SERIES**

King's Dragon

Prince of Dogs

The Burning Stone

Child of Flame

The Gathering Storm

In the Ruins

Crown of Stars

**THE NOVELS OF
THE JARAN**

Jaran

An Earthly Crown

His Conquering Sword

The Law of Becoming

**THE HIGHROAD
TRILOGY**

A Passage of Stars

Revolution's Shore

The Price of Ransom

SERVANT
MAGE

KATE ELLIOTT

A TOM DOHERTY ASSOCIATES BOOK
NEW YORK

This is a work of fiction. All of the characters, organizations, and events
portrayed in this novel are either products of the author's
imagination or are used fictitiously.

SERVANT MAGE

Copyright © 2021 by Katrina Elliott

All rights reserved.

Edited by Lee Harris

A Tordotcom Book
Published by Tom Doherty Associates
120 Broadway
New York, NY 10271

www.tor.com

Tor® is a registered trademark of Macmillan Publishing Group, LLC.

Library of Congress Cataloging-in-Publication Data

Names: Elliott, Kate, 1958– author.
Title: Servant mage / Kate Elliott.
Description: First edition. | New York : Tordotcom, 2022. |
"A Tom Doherty Associates book."
Identifiers: LCCN 2021033447 (print) | LCCN 2021033448 (ebook) |
ISBN 9781250769053 (hardcover) | ISBN 9781250769046 (ebook)
Subjects: GSAFD: Fantasy fiction.
Classification: LCC PS3555.L5917 S47 2022 (print) |
LCC PS3555.L5917 (ebook) | DDC 813/.54—dc23
LC record available at https://lccn.loc.gov/2021033447
LC ebook record available at https://lccn.loc.gov/2021033448

Our books may be purchased in bulk for promotional, educational, or
business use. Please contact your local bookseller or the Macmillan Corporate
and Premium Sales Department at 1-800-221-7945, extension 5442,
or by email at MacmillanSpecialMarkets@macmillan.com.

First Edition: January 2022

Printed in the United States of America

0 9 8 7 6 5 4 3 2 1

To those who light the way

SERVANT MAGE

1

By mid-afternoon the back courtyard of the gentles' wing of the inn lay quiet. The last of the customers departed, having lingered over a fine midday meal in sumptuously decorated dining chambers. While the kitchen staff prepared for suppers that would be served by Lamplight, the boss was either out flattering well-connected suppliers or sequestered in her chamber with a glass of wine and a comfortable couch for a nap.

This interlude made mid-afternoon the best time to clean the fancy privies, according to the boss. That suited Fellian just fine once she'd realized how she could take advantage of the only time no one was directly overseeing her.

She had finished her upstairs chores scrubbing the private dining chambers. Now she carried two buckets from the inn's well into the empty courtyard with its painted walls and flagstone pavement. Three fancy tiled steps led up to the fancy tiled porch with three separate privy doors, each fancifully painted with visions of floral extravagance. After setting down the buckets, one with soapy and one with clear water, she checked the pocket of her faded canvas apron. She had just enough charcoal for today.

She set to sweeping the flagstones, trying to calm her fretful thoughts with the steady scrape of bristles against pavement. Her gaze drifted across the elaborate murals that adorned the courtyard's walls, but she didn't really see them. Would Nish come? Servants never knew when they would be assigned elsewhere, when scraps of freedom would get revoked at the whim of a boss, when new restrictions would be levied by the council so virtuous people need not fear the corrupting power of mages.

The rattle hung on the alley side of the back gate rustled as someone shook it. She hurried over, swung up the crossbar, and cracked open the gate. When a pleasant scent assailed her, she opened the gate a bit more.

Nish's round face greeted her but her usual cheerful smile was creased down into an anxious frown. She clutched a basket against her chest, fragrant bundles of herbs tied and stacked inside.

"I brought someone," she whispered. "You said you could manage a second person now Karry got transferred away."

Fellian took a step outside to look both ways down the alley, a restricted corridor between high, blank walls. To the left the lane bent out of sight around a corner. To the right it ran straight for some ways. No one was in sight in either direction, but a servant on an errand could come along at any moment. "You know what will happen if we're caught."

"I promise he won't rat on us. It's my uncle."

Caution warred with a fierce, reckless desire to poke a defiant pin into the underbelly of the oblivious beast that had destroyed her life. "All right. I trust you."

Nish's frown brightened into a smile. She whistled a

phrase from one of the council-approved songs sung nightly by maudlin drinkers in shabby vulgars' common rooms. About twenty strides to the right, an alcove had been built into the wall. Its lintel was carved with a bundle of five arrows set between two curved cattle horns. Such alcoves appeared at regular intervals along straight paths but were long abandoned to dust. Fellian had no idea what they'd been used for before the revolution. Nish's uncle had used this one to stand out of sight of anyone looking down the straight stretch. He stepped into view and hurried to the gate.

His steps slowed as he looked her over with his one good eye.

"You're just a girl, and a mage too," he said as accusingly as if he'd been assured he'd be meeting with a loyal Liberationist only to be presented with a criminal cabal of Monarchists.

"Uncle!" Nish cast an apologetic glance at Fellian.

"It's all right. I know my letters. I can teach them to you if you wish."

His suspicion wavered as he chewed on his lower lip. "You can teach me to read? Truly?"

"I can. But you have to come inside quick."

Nish tapped the man's arm to bestir him. With a skeptical frown, he came in. His gaze flickered as he took in the porch's tile work, but mostly he gaped at the murals.

The scene spread across three walls depicted the final battle when the forces of reform under the leadership of the August Protector had overthrown the disgraced and corrupt monarchy. Such murals were to be found anywhere people might have to wait their turn and thus have a chance to contemplate the Great Liberation, even in an inn's back courtyard where monied folks took to the privy. The artist had portrayed both sides in vivid colors and stirring emotion: the last dragon queen in her moment of death at the hands of a humble foot soldier whose ditchdigger's shovel hung at his back; the courageous Liberationist troops who fought with purity and righteousness; the stalwart but doomed Monarchist warriors and their legendary champion, the straw-haired barbarian known as Jojen the Wolf, who chose death over dishonor.

Nish's uncle closed his big hands into fists. "This is no schoolroom."

"That's right, it's the courtyard to a privy." Back home, Fellian would have called him "uncle" too, but people didn't appreciate that courtesy here. Still, it grated to have no respectful way to acknowledge his age and whatever accident had scarred his face and ruined his left eye. "We use the steps as a writing board. Do you have your charcoal, Nish? You can show him the letters."

"I know my letters," he said stiffly. "Got them when I was a boy. Then the revolution happened. Recruiters came through town and took us to the army."

He paused, as if waiting for her to ask about his injuries, but she'd learned never to ask. It was better to wait for people to tell you what they wanted you to know.

"Then afterward the councils put us to work. Lost a lot of people to famine. There wasn't time for anything else. Anyway, the August Protector says it is selfishness for hungry folk to ask for luxuries like school. But I never forgot my letters."

"Of course you didn't." Fellian smiled encouragingly. "To start with why don't you write all the letters out for me on the bottom step while I replace the herbs in the privies?"

He glanced toward the courtyard's entrance porch, shaded beneath wide eaves. Closed doors led into the inn. "I can do that. But what if someone comes? If we're caught we'll be thrown in prison."

"There are no customers this time of day. Only customers are allowed to use these privies. I clean, so it's no surprise if people find me here. Nish delivers herbs. After the lesson I scrub off the steps."

He nodded. "That's clever."

Nish fished a rolled-up leaf from her basket and unwrapped it to display three new charcoal sticks. "I roasted these two days ago. Do you want one, Fellian?"

She wanted one so hard it burned, remembering how her mother and fathers had taught her to make charcoal in bulk for writing. But she choked down the sting of tears. "No. You'll need them to practice at home."

Nish handed one of the sticks to her uncle.

Fellian said, "Write out your name first. That's always a good way to begin."

A flash of panic widened his eyes.

As Mother had always said, people learn best when they don't feel ashamed.

"I'm sorry, I forgot your name even though Nish has mentioned you before," Fellian lied.

"Oran."

"Spelled O-R-A-N?"

"That's right!" he said with a sigh of relief, lips mouthing the four letters as he repeated them twice under his breath.

"Can you start with that?"

"Yes, yes. I can start with that." He took a charcoal stick from Nish and knelt at the bottom of the steps, staring at the flat surface as if it were a poisonous toad. He sucked in a breath, then laboriously began to write in distorted but recognizable strokes, first the letters of his name and then the parade of letters that was the staple of every schoolroom.

"You watch over him, Nish. Teaching others is the best way to learn."

Fellian took the basket from Nish and went to the first privy door. Inside, a polished wooden seat with a lid kept the worst of the stench down, but to keep up the high ranking of her establishment the boss had a deal with Nish's herbalist boss for a fresh delivery of strong-smelling herbs every other day.

At each stall Fellian crumbled the withered previous bundle into the lime-whitened pit before placing a vibrant new bundle into a wire basket. Afterward she swept the courtyard and scrubbed the porch, all the while keeping up an exchange with Nish: new words to spell, long phrases she wrote out for Nish to read aloud. Oran doggedly worked on writing out a parade of letters, over and over, with the tenacity of a man who has fought his way back from the cliff of despair.

Nish was wiping off words to give herself space to write again when Oran went still. His hand, scratching out a letter, halted. He looked toward the doors that led into the inn.

"Someone is coming," he said in a low, frightened voice. "More than one person."

Fellian heard nothing except distant street traffic: the grind of wheels, the clop of hooves, a wagoner's shout.

He got to his feet with some trouble; his left leg didn't straighten easily. "Nish, we best go. Hustle up."

Nish grabbed the charcoal out of his hand and the basket off the porch. "He's never wrong." Her drawn expression shouted its own message as her gaze dropped to the mage's badge Fellian wore.

Oran flushed. "It's not like that," he said in the tone of a man who's been caught out.

"No, of course not," said Fellian, knowing exactly what he was hiding and why he didn't want a servant mage indentured to the government to know. All those born with mage gifts owed them to the liberation. They weren't to be selfishly hoarded for private gain. Any who tried to hide their gift would see their families imprisoned as punishment for not reporting to the authorities. Afterward, of course, the discovered mage would be bound into service anyway.

"Hurry," she added, abruptly out of breath as she considered what would happen to her if it was ever discovered she'd known and hadn't reported him.

She followed them to the gate, let them out, barred it, and ran back to the steps. Cheeks hot, hands shaking, she dropped to her knees and began scrubbing away the damning letters that had been so methodically written onto the lowest step.

A door into the inn slid open.

2

A young man stepped onto the portico. When his gaze settled on her he tensed, but as he took her measure his shoulders relaxed.

He sauntered into the courtyard. His spotless blue tunic with interlocking winged snakes embroidered down the sleeves marked him as an Adept, a mage whose gift was not commonplace as most were but superior and thus laudable and demanding of the highest respect. She knew better than to test the patience of such a man, especially when he set a polished boot on the first step, close enough to kick her.

After running a cloth over the damp steps to wipe away any last trace of charcoal, she sat back on her heels to get out of his way.

He examined her with the same look she imagined he would give a stain on the floor of any chamber he was required to frequent. But he didn't climb the steps to the privy. Instead he ostentatiously turned his head to study the murals. He had all the time in the worlds and nothing urgent to be bothered about. She, of course, was required to get the cleaning done before dusk, when her Lamplighting duties started.

"These are strikingly good murals." Since there was no one

9

else in the courtyard it seemed the Adept was addressing her. "Better than the official ones at the government offices in Exculpation Square, don't you think?"

No one who was wise answered such a question. Anyway, she was struck by the way he had taken exactly the stance of one of the Monarchist soldiers, chin lifted, shoulders square. He might have been the actual model for the figure except his glossy raven-black hair was cut in the short liberator style rather than grown long and woven into a five-strand Monarchist braid.

"Or do you think at all? Regardless of their artistic merit they are certainly considerably cleaner than the murals in Exculpation Square." He looked at the brush in her hands. "That's a lot of time spent scrubbing that might be better used for more productively liberating chores."

Good-looking men in particular annoyed her, so she said, in her most innocent tone, "If the gentles' privy is too clean for your comfort, there's a vulgars' latrine in the commons courtyard. It's only scrubbed once a month instead of daily, if that suits your preferences."

He smiled with what was surely malicious glee. "I was searching for something I've been told was eliminated last year from the servants' asylum in Alabaster City and assigned here. I think that would be . . . *you*."

A sick fear crashed through her heart. Air curdled in her lungs. Head down, she dipped the brush into the soapy bucket and set to vigorously scrubbing the side of the stairs.

"I just work here, Your Eminence. The boss takes all questions of that kind."

"Now you are all politeness."

"I have to finish cleaning before twilight, if you don't mind, Your Eminence."

"I have a job for a servant mage named Fellian who I am told is a creditable Lamplighter. Young and attractive, although why my informant would bother to note that detail I couldn't tell you."

Her head came up sharply. His crooked smile was back. She wondered if she could scour it off his face with the brush's stiff bristles.

"Although maybe you could tell me," he added.

She was tempted to put a hand on his beautiful boot and scorch it. "How could I tell you since I have no idea who your informant is?"

His smile widened. "That's not important. I need a Lamplighter. I'll pay well, and arrange for all necessary clearances from your boss."

Don't do it, whispered a murmur of caution in her soul while another part of her thrilled like a bird opening its wings at long last.

"It's an impressive offer," she temporized. Her traitorous heart raced with possibility, with chance. With terrible, painful, cursed hope.

"So you *are* Fellian?"

"It might be worth my while to be, if you offer a big enough payment."

He took his handsome boot off the step and snapped his fingers. Four soldiers wearing dull green Liberationist uniforms emerged from the inn.

She glanced toward the back gate, gauging how fast she could get there and out, then looked at the sky to estimate how soon it would be dark. She had an advantage at night they didn't know about.

"There was a third quality the headmaster mentioned: the distinctive aroma of fever grass. Night can't hide you from me now I've taken a taste of that strong smell. Do you want to tell me what your obsession with fever grass is?"

"No."

She set the brush upside down on the ground and stood. He wasn't much taller than she was, and not physically intimidating. In another life she would have shoved him to the ground and bolted. But he was an Adept, not a mere servant mage. To assault him would land her in a viler prison than the indenture she suffered now. Worse, since he was an Air Adept, his threat to track her down if she tried to run wasn't bombast.

Anyway, she couldn't run. That was just the dream she plagued herself with: that she would escape indenture and return home across half the country without a travel license, money, or supplies.

"What's the pay?" Rumor whispered it was possible to buy a travel license on the black market. She'd learned to be ruthlessly pragmatic. It was how she'd survived the last five years.

"That these dutiful soldiers don't throw you in prison for being the daughter of executed criminals."

She clenched her hands into fists to choke a rush of panic. "You and I both know whatever an Adept like you accuses me of, the council will back you up. Does it ever bother you that your lies are treated better than the truth?"

He cocked his head to one side. A ray of afternoon sun glinted on the shiny gold of an ear cuff, a flicker of light that got in her eyes and made her blink. "Do you think you can do anything about it?"

"Of course a servant mage like me can't do anything about it."

"Then why do you speak words that can get you executed?"

"Because you made me an offer. If you were working on the orders of the Liberationist Council you'd have marched in and handed a transfer license to my boss to take control of my indenture. So I'm guessing this is something you're doing for yourself. Or maybe on hire for someone you can't refuse. Someone who is paying you a fee that allows you to afford those expensive clothes. I hope you've budgeted hush money. My boss will turn you in if she sees profit in it. She's like that."

The Adept glanced skyward as if the air was speaking to him, and maybe it was. A flash of irritation crossed his elegant features, making Fellian want to congratulate the air. When he noticed her smirk, his expression hardened. Indenture had given her good instincts for the moods of people who had power over her. He was hiding something, so she decided to push.

"If you tracked down the likes of me, you must be scraping the bottom of the barrel. Give me half up front and I won't cause trouble."

"You won't cause trouble if you value your life," he muttered, but the words had a peevish quality that made her want to laugh. Although she schooled her expression he saw a hint of mockery on her face. He turned to the soldiers. "Bring her."

"I have to fetch a few things from my bunk."

"We will provide all the gear you need for where we're going."

"I am sure I'll thank you for it. But if you don't want my Lamp to fail on a moonless night in the middle of whatever life-threatening mission you have planned, you'll let me fetch a few things from my bunk."

"No questions about the mission?"

"Would you tell me if I asked?"

He arched an eyebrow in a supercilious expression that would have cowed her into silence at the beginning of the conversation.

But she'd gotten a guess at his weaknesses by now. "I didn't think so. I know your type."

"What type is that?"

"The type who's never had to take responsibility for another's well-being, not even his own."

By the flare of his very pretty eyes she could see she had startled him. His jaw tightened.

She stuck out a hand, palm up. "I want payment in coin. Ten argents per day you expect us to be gone, to be deposited in a bank under my name with a codicil that assigns the coin to me without reference to my indenture. That's so my boss and the chancery can't take it from me."

She'd never get that rate, but even one argent a day would give her a nest egg to build on.

His frown this time looked more considering than hostile. Before he could speak, the shortest of the soldiers handed her a heavy pouch. Since the day she was torn from her home Fellian had survived by reading the emotions of others while concealing her own, but it was impossible not to gasp when she looked inside. She had never seen so many argents jostling together in her entire life, yet he hadn't even bargained any more than you would over a modest supper of bread and cheese.

He smiled as gloatingly as if he'd just won a victory. "I'll make the arrangements with your boss and the bank while you fetch your things," he said with a glance toward the privy as if insinuating her bunk was inside. He held out a hand.

Reluctantly she handed back the pouch. "What's your name? You know mine."

"I like the sound of 'Your Eminence.' Haolu will accompany you."

Thus dismissed, Fellian headed for the gate that led into the old stable yard. Haolu was the shortest soldier, a stocky young woman with a stolid expression and a gaze that flicked restlessly all around as if she was sure a rogue demon-wraith was about to slither out from a rift in earth or air.

The establishment at which Fellian worked had once been a well-appointed lodging house that served only nobles and their retinues. After the change of government and its ban on unrestricted travel, the lodging rooms had been turned into fancy private dining rooms for monied private parties. A noisy, smoky, rundown common room had been made available for the locals from the surrounding district to show all were equal under the law. The extensive stable had been turned into housing for indentured servants and convicts serving out labor sentences. Some worked at the establishment while others were hired out by the local chancery to offices and businesses.

Haolu followed her past a faded cloth curtain into a narrow stall fitted with a three-tiered bunk bed. The woman sniffed and said, "Fever grass, eh? Repels bugs, doesn't it?"

Fellian flashed her a surprised look.

"I'm not council-born like he is." The soldier studied the top bunk. "What's the light?"

Fellian climbed up to her bunk. Every morning she rolled her meager possessions into her blanket and wrapped the bundle with a cord, ready to sling across her back in case she got a chance to run. Every morning she shaped a fist-sized ball of fire, sealed it with a glass-like exterior into a Lamp as she'd been taught at the asylum, and stretched that Lamp until it became glowing wire. This cord of light she wrapped around the bundle to prevent thieves from stealing it while she was at work.

She pressed a hand onto the hot pulse of the Lamp and absorbed the magic back into the demon-wraith that nested in her bones. A scent of burning stung the air before fading. After her hand cooled she gathered up two faded sachets and a fresh bundle of fever grass and climbed down with the blanket slung over her back.

"You're not bringing those herbs, are you?" asked Haolu.

"I hate bugs." She shuddered. The sweaty odor off the other bunks smelled stronger now she was leaving. It was horrifying to imagine having to return here and crawl up that ladder back into the grind of daily existence she'd have to endure for at least eight more years.

The soldier studied her in a blunt way that made Fellian take a step back. She found herself caught with the rough wood of the lower and middle bunk pressed into her calves and shoulders, forced into a corner.

"I was like you once," said Haolu. "The chancery took me from my family at the census festival. Sent me to an asylum. They wouldn't let us bathe or wash our clothes for three months. Did they do that to you too?"

Fellian shrugged a shoulder, the most answer she was willing to give. She could still feel the sensation of bugs crawling on her skin at night when she had lain shivering on the filthy bunks of an overcrowded asylum, listening to the other mage-gifted children crying in misery and fear.

Haolu fixed her gaze on the rolled-up blanket tucked against Fellian's hip. "You got a knife hidden in there. How'd you manage that?"

There was no possible way Haolu could have seen the knife concealed inside the blanket roll. A cold certainty squeezed her heart.

"You're earth-fettered. The Adept is air. So are the other two water and aether in disguise as soldiers, like you? A five-arrow quiver is illegal."

Haolu nodded calmly. "You took the money. You're part of a five-arrow quiver now. If we're caught, you'll be executed with the rest of us."

"Why me?"

"I don't know. The Old Man chose you."

Footsteps clapped from the stable aisle. Haolu glanced over her shoulder, listening as whoever it was walked past. With encroaching dusk, the laborers were starting to come home.

Haolu unwound her green sash and stripped off her uniform jacket to reveal a second sash and jacket beneath. She tossed it on the bunk and drew a knife from her belt.

"Wear the uniform to hide your servant's jacket. First we cut your hair."

"Cut my hair?" In a heart-pounding rush, Fellian realized this was it and she hadn't seen it coming. "There is no bank payment and no license, is there? You're stealing me."

"Move it."

She knelt on the floor and took down her hair with a sense of foreboding. Haolu took hold of its length midway down her back, twisted it to pull it taut, and sheared it off at the neck. As Fellian tugged on the uniform jacket, Haolu rolled the hair into a length of faded silk and tucked it into her pouch so no trace of Fellian was left.

The weight of her head changed, in some ways lightened and in others thrown off balance. Whatever happened next she'd never return to this bunk. She'd escape, or she'd die.

3

On the side streets, food stalls were doing a brisk business with the after-work rush. Fellian and Haolu blended into the flow, two more soldiers in uniform knee-length jackets.

"Will I get paid, or will His Eminence turn me over to a chancery for a reward after he's gotten what he needs?"

"Hush."

The town wall loomed. Ahead lay the massive gate through which the high nobles had once entered and left the city. The pair of sinewy dragons twined together to make the gate's lintel had years ago had their heads, wings, and legs chipped out. These days the headless "worms" made an entrance for merchants and carters.

Her mouth went dry as they joined a line of people waiting to cross under the gate. "I'm not allowed to leave the town walls. The chancery will add a year onto my indenture if I'm caught—"

"March with shoulders back. Look people right in the eye. Got it?"

Haolu slipped two gate tokens from a pocket sewn onto her sleeve. When their turn came she strode fearlessly up to the sentries. She handed the tokens to a weary-looking older man who wore a servant mage's patchwork jacket just like the ragged one concealed beneath Fellian's borrowed uniform. His was embroidered with a wavy stripe. He weighed the tokens in his right hand, testing their veracity with his water magic.

Fellian clasped her hands behind her back, squeezing her fingers together until the pain distracted her from the yammering in her head that kept screaming at her to give herself up before it was too late. If she turned herself in now, she might only get a year's demerits. Or she might hang like her parents while a paid crowd of celebrants jeered and those who had known the accused stood at the back of the crowd and tried not to condemn themselves by weeping.

It had been too late the moment she'd left the inn without permission.

One of the sentries spoke up. "You're with the Second Deliverance Regiment? How's the fight going in the Iron Hills against Lord Roake and his filthy rebels?"

"No filth that can't be cleaned up in a month," said Haolu as she accepted the tokens back from the water mage. "Lots of abandoned mines to clear out. Worse luck for us. They say there's demons caught in those mines."

The sentry gave Fellian a somber nod. "May you have good fortune, comrades."

Fellian held her breath as she and Haolu passed under the ruined dragon lintel and through a dim passageway that pierced the thick wall. She kept listening for the boss to come running, shouting her name, but all she heard was the end-of-day trumpet giving its last call before sunset curfew.

Haolu kept walking at an unconcerned pace down a packed-earth ramp that funneled them into the outer district. The haphazard sprawl of tenements, manufactories, and stables was home to folk who couldn't afford to live inside the stone walls of the inner city. Out here the streets still teemed with foot traffic. Loud soldiers traveled in packs like hungry dogs. Free laborers pulled carts piled high with crated chickens, bags stamped with the icon for millet, and baskets of soap.

"Stop jumping at every noise. You look suspicious. There's no curfew here."

"The boss will be looking for me, wondering why I'm not lighting Lamps. They'll call an alarm and shut the gates in the outer palisade. We can't possibly reach the palisade gates before we're trapped. They search street by street—"

"Stop mewling like a frightened whelp. He said you'd be tougher than this. But I guess I was right, wasn't I?"

"Who said I'd be tougher than this?"

"Hush."

Haolu directed her down an alley and through the back entrance of a large inn. A lively roar of conversation and laughter swelled out from a common room opening onto the rear courtyard. Under a thatched shelter people were filling up pitchers of drink from liquid simmering in big kettles.

By going up steps to a second level they came to a quiet room where two men sat on opposite sides of a table setting out a game of Four Seasons on a checkered board. It took her a moment to recognize the Adept, who had stripped off his expensive tunic. Like an excited child he was carefully setting down miniature playing pieces—shovels, plows, scythes, and knives—in their appropriate starting places on the board. The older man sitting opposite glanced up to mark their entrance, his expression offering no hint of welcome.

When Haolu nodded at him Fellian realized he was one of the soldiers, although his posture and the gravity of his expression suggested he wasn't the common trooper his single-striped sleeve said he was.

The Adept looked up with an audible sniff. "For the love of mercy, please take her to the baths."

"We have to get out of here before my boss alerts the constables and they close the palisade gates," said Fellian. "Don't you understand anything?"

"I understand we have a plan. The first part of the plan is that you not stink." His eyes and nose were already watering.

"Here." She dumped the three bundles of fever grass in the middle of the board, displacing the playing pieces.

The Adept covered his nose and mouth with a handkerchief and sneezed. "Even this can't cover the stench of the privy. People ought to wash more."

"Does it possibly occur to you that indentured servants like me are only allowed to bathe twice a month? Even then we add a day to our service for the privilege."

He sat back with such sharp surprise that his arm accidentally swept playing pieces off the board to clatter on the plank floor. "Add a *day*? For a *bath*?"

She blinked about ten times before cudgeling her exasperation back into the pit where she kept all the emotions she would suffer demerits for letting out. "Don't you know anything about how mage indenture works? Our labor is our payment *and* our debt."

His shoulders tensed as his jaw tightened. Instead of answering he bent over to pick up the fallen game pieces.

The older man glanced toward Haolu and tipped his head toward the door.

"Come on." Haolu hustled Fellian out of the small room, down the stairs, and through a gloomy bricked-in corridor toward the smell of scented soaps marinating in hot water. In a low voice she added, "Don't annoy the Old Man."

"That's the old man? He's not that old, not old like my grandmother. You say it like it's a title. Isn't he a trooper like you?"

Haolu laughed curtly. "Over here."

Here was a long line of private bathing rooms set up as curtained stalls along an outdoor walkway. A tall figure leaned against the wall, watching for them, and straightened up to reveal the last soldier. This person also looked old enough to be Fellian's parent, with a sun-weathered face but without the streaks of silver in black hair that the older man had.

"I'm Invi. There's a uniform and soap inside."

"And no way to sneak out the back," added Haolu.

"Don't worry," said Fellian. "I'm well aware I'm trapped if I don't cooperate. If I go to the constabulary and claim the Adept is a criminal, he and you lot will all say I'm lying. We know how that will go for me."

"Smart girl, isn't she?" muttered Haolu with a sarcastic skyward glance.

"Here, now, Lulu, cut her some slack. You've had a taste of what she's been through." Invi had eyes so bright a blue they shone as they examined Fellian. "I'll trim that ragged cut when we get out of town."

"It's illegal for servant mages to cut their hair," Fellian said.

"Strangely enough we are aware of that. Go in."

"But—"

"Don't worry. We have a plan. But you smell. I mean no insult by saying so, given the conditions under which you labor. It's a quick tell. We need to get you clean so an Air Adept brought in to sniff your bunk can't follow us."

A hundred questions crowded Fellian's mind but instead she went into the bathing stall. Haolu and Invi followed her, closing the entry curtain behind them for privacy. Of course it was dark, so she shaped a ball of light, sealed it, and placed it on an iron holder fixed to the wall.

"Skilled work," said Invi.

The praise warmed Fellian though it also made her suspicious, alert for the smile and slap the preceptors would give to student mages they felt were getting above themselves.

Haolu gave the Lamp a skeptical glance, handed Invi the hair rolled up in silk, and went out.

Invi said, "Can't have anyone finding this braid and wondering where it came from. Human hair is also good for bowstrings, sutures, and traps for wraiths."

"Traps? The only way to trap a demon-wraith is to fetter it in a human body. Like us."

"Such lies! We are not fettered. Our soul-wraiths aren't demons. The Liberationist academies teach you poor children nothing but lies." Invi held up the still intact braid and sniffed it. "Whew! It really stinks of fever grass."

"It keeps off the bugs and lice. Are you an escaped servant mage too?"

"If you young ones were being taught properly, you'd know the eyes of a water mage don't get a shine until we reach the Adept level of mastery." The icy gleam of Invi's eyes was more noticeable in the dim room.

"So you're virtuously born too? A gentle like His Eminence?"

"Like *His Eminence*?" Deft fingers untangled the braid. "I like your sense of humor, girl. We'll never let him live that title down."

"Isn't he properly titled 'eminence'? He seems like he comes from a council household."

"Oh, he does. But I don't. So don't use it on me."

"But only gentles and eminences have the capacity to be trained as Adepts. That's why they are born into council households."

"Is that what they teach you? Shame on them! Adept is just a name for a higher level of training. It has nothing to do with where you are born or who you are born to. Anyone can become an Adept if they have the discipline. If they are allowed to study beyond apprentice level, as you young ones have not been."

Fellian thought of the skills she had learned in secret, on her own, and said nothing, but Invi's words woke the worm of rebellion sleeping in her heart. "Are you saying it used to be different?"

Invi frowned. "It's disgraceful what's been done to the mage orders. Before, every person was brought into a mage ward as an apprentice, not as an indentured child raised to become a servant subject to the council's whim or a boss's whip. Mages were respected guild members who could gain as much skill as they were willing to work for."

"You don't look old enough to remember the liberation."

"Water makes a mage stay smooth long after others harden into wrinkles." Invi dunked the cut hair into a basin of water and squeezed lemon juice over it. "We'll let this sit. Be quick, but wash everything. Get as much scent off you and your old clothes as you can."

After Invi went out, Fellian stripped. It was cold enough, midway through the season of scythes, that dumping a bucket of cold water over her head made her gasp. But it was glorious to scrub herself with a sweet-smelling lavender soap, to rinse until she couldn't smell fever grass. She was made anew, like being reborn. Shivering, she reveled in this unbelievable chance to thoroughly wash her grimy servants' clothing, to unroll her blanket and wash it along with her winter cap and spare under-tunic, and even scrub some of the stiff staining from the drawers she crammed rags into for her bleeding although it had been months since her last one. She also cleaned her spoon, bowl, and the precious cracked ebony comb that was the last thing she had left of Older Father. Only the knife she'd pilfered from a drunken customer who'd passed out in the privy lay untouched, its aether-honed steel still bright. She'd stolen it because it reminded her of home.

"What's taking so long?" Haolu asked from the other side of the curtain.

"Getting the smell of fever grass off everything so it doesn't trouble His Eminence."

Invi snorted a laugh, then said, "Go get something to eat, Lulu. That curdled frown of yours is killing my enjoyment of the fresh air."

To dry off with a clean towel rather than a grimy shared one was an unheard-of luxury. Afterward she dressed in blessedly clean and apparently never-worn undergarments and a warm wool uniform of jacket, sash, and wrap trousers. Her uniform included gloves, a fur-lined military cap with ear flaps, and sturdy leather boots with genuine socks instead of scraps of old cloth to wrap around her feet to keep out the cold. It was too much to take in.

In a shaken voice she said, through the curtain, "Do I leave the towel?"

Invi swept past the curtain, squeezed out the hair, wrapped it in the wet silk, and brushed fingers along the curve of the basin to capture any stray hairs. "The bucket, trough, and stool belong to the establishment, nothing else. There's a waxed leather pouch to put the soap in. Do the boots fit?"

"Yes, of course," she said immediately, even though they were too big.

She rolled everything up into the blanket, then was so dizzied by a wave of light-headedness that she had to take a few breaths while on her hands and knees before she could stand. After absorbing her Lamp she went out with the damp blanket roll slung over her back. Invi looked her up and down in the light of Lamps made by some other toiling servant mage.

"Are you sure the boots fit? If they don't we'll get you a different pair when we can."

Fellian bit her lip.

"I promise," Invi added.

She let out a nervous breath. "They're too big. I can cram cloth in. It will be fine."

"Lulu said the same. You poor children. It's terrible how little you expect. You deserve boots that fit."

The Water Adept escorted Fellian back to the chamber. Both the Air Adept and the fever grass were missing from the room. The two men had about finished their game. The older man had his absent opponent boxed into a corner and was waiting for him to return for the final blow. Haolu was shoveling millet porridge into her mouth. Invi gestured to the side table where a bowl of porridge sat next to a platter of chicken fried up with leeks and a squad of dumplings whose aroma made Fellian's mouth water.

"How much may I have?" she asked awkwardly.

The older man looked up with a frown so stark she wanted to sink into the floor out of shame.

Invi sighed. "It's all for you, Felli. Do you mind if I call you Felli? I had a cousin named Fellian and that's what we called her."

"It's all for me?"

"If she eats that much rich food she'll throw it up, won't she?" said Haolu. "I'll take the dumplings."

The fragrance of pepper and turmeric was so rich it untethered Fellian. She stuck out a hand to catch herself against the wall, overcome by a sense of terror she couldn't explain.

The older man stood, took hold of her wrist, and closed his eyes. The grip of his callused fingers was firm without being crushing. She dared not move. He was evidently an aether mage, a diagnostician able to seek out and identify illness within a person's body, even though no mage, however powerful, could heal.

After a few slow breaths, he opened his eyes and released her.

"Sit here," he commanded in a tone she could not disobey.

She sat in the chair he'd vacated. He swept the game pieces into a pouch, folded up the board, then set the food in front of her and, after a brief consideration, left her all the porridge but only two dumpling and a small portion of chicken.

"She's badly undernourished," he said to Invi. "Haolu's right. We'll have to ease her back into a normal ration."

Fellian stared at the food.

Invi smiled sadly. "Chew slowly. But start now. We'll go when Shey returns."

She popped a dumpling into her mouth. As the moist cabbage melded with the flavors of garlic and ginger hit her tongue, tears flooded her cheeks. The aroma and texture were an arrow shot to the heart, an agonizing memory of Older Father frying a pan of dumplings for their supper while Grandmother, Mother, and Younger Father sat at the table writing slogans and messages on strips of wood. *When you're older you can help us, Little Flower,* Younger Father had said to her. *Keep up your practice until you've mastered a council hand that can't be traced.*

The door banged open. The Adept strode in with a fresh swagger and the damp hands and face of someone who has just used the privy and had the luxury to tidy up properly. He was now wearing a soldier's drab uniform, although he looked far too pretty to be a soldier.

"I want a rematch!" he proclaimed to the older man, then saw her sitting at the table. His eyes widened as he took in her clean face, hair, and clothing.

Haolu snickered.

Invi said, kindly, "Close your mouth, Your Eminence, or catch flies. Your choice."

Flushing, he grabbed a dumpling off the platter and popped it in his mouth, chewed, swallowed. "The food's not what a person should become accustomed to, I grant you, but surely it's not bad enough to make you cry."

Fellian swallowed her dumpling and, with it, the last of the caution that had kept her silent this long. She considered them each in turn but it was the older man she addressed. "What's our real mission? I'm tainted by association now, so you may as well tell me so I can be prepared."

"Bad move," said Haolu.

The Air Adept froze, as if he'd sensed a lightning strike about to obliterate them.

Invi closed the door. "If you ask me—"

"She didn't ask you," said the older man. "And now is not the time. Are you ready, Shey?" he asked the Adept.

"Yes, my lord." Realizing he'd made a slip of the tongue, the Adept winced, and glanced at her.

Fellian smirked. "Like I hadn't already guessed you must be Monarchists, with your five-arrow quiver of mages."

"Enough!" The older man's eyes were brown; a silver-colored circle like a sliver of a ring marked off the iris from the pupil. She honestly wasn't sure what this mark portended, if it was the glimmering tail of the demon-wraith that lived inside him. Whatever it was, it could be nothing good. All aether mages, whether servant or Adept, were required by law to serve the council directly and could not be hired out like the others. He was a renegade.

His uncanny gaze held her. "Cooperate and, if we succeed, you will receive the money. If we don't succeed, you will suffer the same fate as we do. Do you understand?"

Anger lit her tongue. "I understand you're using me, just as the chancery and my boss do. That you've made it impossible for me to go back."

"Why would you want to go back to servitude? When we discovered your history we thought you would support us."

She ate the second dumpling, savoring its richness as the others waited for her to finish and speak. "Do you know why my parents were arrested and executed?"

"For sedition, against their local council," he said. "It's why we picked you."

"So you have access to chancery records. That's interesting. And you thought I would hate the Liberationists. As I do. But why should I trust *you*?"

He placed an open hand, fingers spread, to his chest in the loyalty salute that had been banned since the death of the last monarch. "I give you my oath, which I swear on the memory of my ancestors, of my queen and the monarchs I serve, and on my honor. If we survive this mission, you will walk away unharmed, with money and the freedom to go where you wish without our interference."

He had an aura of honor about him that reminded her of the doomed Monarchist soldiers in the mural. But that didn't mean she wasn't going to bargain, as her grandmother had taught her.

"I'll agree if you can also provide me with a travel license and identity papers."

He looked at Invi, who nodded. "Invi can manage it."

Impossible not to exult. She bit down a grin, trying to act calm. "Very well. I'm in."

4

Instead of heading down into the courtyard, Shey led them up the stairs into a third-floor attic. Fellian shaped a Lamp so they could weave their way through a musty space crammed with locked chests. They halted at a ladder. While she held the light at the base of the ladder, Shey, Invi, and Haolu climbed up. She wondered what would happen if, after the older man went up, she didn't follow.

Behind her, he said, "Douse the Lamp and go up."

"Don't you need it to see?"

The silver ring in his eyes shone like a sliver of hope in darkness. "I take the rearguard, Fellian. You'll learn that about me."

She wanted to ask his name but knew he would not tell her. "Yes, my lord," she said, to test his reaction.

"Use the title Captain, if you must. Go."

She absorbed the Lamp and, in darkness, climbed. The roof had a gentle slope, making it feasible to balance on the curved tiles. From up here the distant watch-fires that marked the outer palisades glowed like restless fire demons trapped atop towers. Gleaming orbs shaped by fire mages like herself shone where gates in the town wall had been shut for the night. Stars glittered overhead as if a thousand thousand Lamps had been hung and then forgotten by weary servant mages required to stay on call all night lest someone with a curfew token needed their services to light them from a late-night supper with friends back to a luxurious home. Her stomach churned, made uneasy by the rich food. The captain climbed up behind her and closed the hatch door.

"Shhh." Shey tipped a hand to his ear, a movement she saw as the heat of his body shifting position.

Through trial and error and with patience, she'd taught herself the skill of discerning heat at night even though it wasn't part of the curriculum at the asylum. Servant mages who housed fire were trained to kindle and tend hearth-fires, stoves, and manufactory kilns, and to shape Lamps against the dark. That was all.

Out of the silence spoke a voice she ought not to have been able to hear. Air Adepts had the skill to pull sound to them off the air, which is why the council employed them as scouts and spies. *"It's thought she stole a soldier's uniform and has accomplices. Monarchist rebels who sneaked into town. They can't have reached the palisade gates yet. We've got an Adept following her smell."*

She elbowed Haolu. "Why are we stuck up here on a roof?"

"Hush."

"But—?"

"Can you not stop with the questions?"

The captain said, quietly, "Surely you know the only skill the liberation allows a servant air mage to learn is that of seven-league boots."

"That only works in daytime and when you can see where you're going."

Shey coughed. "So says the servant fire mage in her infinite wisdom. Anyway, I can see where I'm going." He turned to face one of the distant watch-fires.

From the courtyard of the inn below a voice raised. "Everyone! Sit down and don't move! We are looking for a fugitive."

Shey extended his arms, backs of his hands touching and palms facing out. It was as if his fingers peeled away the air itself to reveal a blot of darkness behind it. The darkness undulated, as opaque as densest silk and with an uncanny shimmer like it might be alive and breathing. He pulled his arms wide to create a gap like a slitted cat's eye, narrowest at top and bottom and as wide through the middle as the wingspan of his arms.

Invi stepped into the gap and vanished. Fellian gaped, because it was impossible.

"But you have to be able to see—"

Haolu shoved her forward. Stumbling, she hit a pressure so cold her eyes hurt, then sucked in what felt like a lungful of sand-scorched air, and rammed into Invi's back. She coughed raggedly.

From below, in darkness, a voice said, "Did you hear something?"

She clapped a hand over her mouth to stifle a yelp of surprise. Invi yanked her to one side as Haolu stepped out, then Shey, and last of all the captain as the Eye slid shut behind them. Heat blasted the left side of her face. They stood atop a watchtower, a small square platform that surrounded two massive iron vats. One was a-rumble with flames to mark that all was well, the roads were open, and the land at peace.

Shey stood at a metal railing peering into the night beyond the palisade. Far away, just at the edge of the blue-black horizon, burned another watch-fire. Its distant tower marked the south road toward Alabaster City, which lay a month's journey away for folk who had to walk.

"I heard something thump up there," said one guard nervously to another down below. "We'd best investigate. They say Lord Roake's rebels can fly."

"And they say the soup at the mess hall has meat in it. It was just the wind. Or your wind. Whew! That smell! Anyway, no one's been up the ladder since we took watch."

"You laugh, but my old granddad saw all kinds of things when he fought in the border wars. Before the Liberationists, I mean. Mages who could steal the face of another person. Mages who could call lightning from the sky. Mages who could walk through demonland and call wraiths into the world to devour people."

"Just because a tale is told by old folks don't make it true. My old granddad said he swam the Eldorian Torrent when he was a young man, but he drowned in a pond on a windless day when he fell out of his boat while fishing. Couldn't swim a lick. Still, let's say it's true Lord Roake's rebels can fly. I'm not climbing up. You go if you're so keen on checking. It's your turn to feed the fire, isn't it?"

"Go," whispered the captain.

Shey peeled open another Eye. They stepped through again.

Braced for it, Fellian held her breath through the sand-scorched passage. As she stumbled against Invi, she inhaled a stinging cloud of smoke. Her eyes streamed as she doubled over, trying not to cough.

Haolu thumped her on the back and murmured in her ear, "We're climbing down."

Short of breath from the smoke that seared in her chest, she groped her way down a ladder. Its rungs descended alongside a pulley stitched with baskets filled with pitch-streaked firewood. Once her boots touched glorious earth she stood with eyes closed, trying to calm her hammering heart. Invi tucked a hand under her elbow and guided her out from beneath the scaffolding. On the other side of the fire-tower stood a fortified house where fire-tenders lived.

A branch snapped under Fellian's boot. They all froze. The captain placed himself between their line and the fire-tenders' house. His hand rested on his sword's hilt with the ease of a person who knows how to fight. Someone inside was playing a mournful fiddle tune, and the melody never faltered.

"Go," he whispered.

The tower was surrounded by a square of packed dirt

and beyond this by fields. They walked in silence along a cart path that led away from the main road toward the woods. A quarter moon was rising. An owl glided past.

The path continued into the woodland, which was relentlessly being chopped away for firewood to feed the watchtower's signal fire. Once they were safely out of sight Fellian shaped a small Lamp and split it into two orbs each the size of a fist, pushing one globe ahead of her and letting the other drift behind. The soft tramp of their feet settled her jangling nerves. The bracing autumn scent of decaying leaves and a kiss of ice on her brow woke her up as sharply as if she had startled awake at long last from a nightmare in which two of her beloved parents had been hanged and she indentured as a servant of the state.

She pushed up to walk alongside Shey. "What did you do with the fever grass?"

"What do you think I did with it? I dumped it in the privy. They'll have to clean out the whole thing to make sure you're not hiding down there."

He and Invi and Haolu laughed.

"Silence," the captain said, so she couldn't say what she wanted to say, that it wasn't the Liberationist soldiers who would be ordered to do the nasty cleaning but an already overworked servant.

They walked as the moon rose, its light shining along the cart path as if the path had been cut through the forest to accommodate the moon's angle of rising at this exact time of year. A glint from the captain's eyes flashed back from the path as if they walked on a ribbon of moonlight of his creation rather than on a rutted dirt track. She wanted to ask how any path could be cut so straight but dared not break the silence, so she was left to turn and turn her own thoughts.

Long ago, in ancient days, the dragons who ruled in the heavens had taken human form and descended to a land plagued by demonic wraiths who blew in storms across the land. They had leashed the demons and fettered them into humankind so they could not infest the land. Some claimed they acted for the good of all while others said the dragons were demons themselves, the worst demons of all, who used the fear and burden of demon-wraiths to chain their subjects.

As the moon reached zenith the sky began to lighten. Her legs ached but she knew better than to complain. In a glade they halted to share a flask of cider and thick slices of bread smeared with buttery goat cheese. The forest spread endlessly onward, the path an old straight track falling endlessly as down a passage whose tapestried walls were the gold and orange and red leaves of autumn. Some distance ahead a broken branch had cracked to form a wedge across the road, visible as dawn brought light to the world.

Now, finally, Shey again deployed the gates of air Fellian had watched young air mages learn at the asylum. It was a skill servant mages used to assist government officials, soldiers, and the virtuous wealthy to travel more quickly than anyone else could. He pulled open an Eye centered on the cracked branch, and they stepped through to arrive beside it. In one step they had walked a hundred. On they traveled, Shey opening gates wherever there was a clear line of sight and a landmark he could capture within the Eye.

By mid-morning she guessed they had covered the distance soldiers would march in a day. Even so, she began to flag. Under the overhanging branches of an oak tree, chilled by the shade, she bent over, hands on knees, to steady herself from a wave of light-headedness.

"Just a little farther, Fellian," the captain said. "Can you make it?"

"Just a little farther and then what?" She stared at the intense red of fallen oak leaves spread on the ground like the promise of a blood-soaked death. "When do I get to know where we're going, and what exactly you need me for? Or for that matter, who you really are?"

He said nothing.

She straightened to look him in the face. "The Iron Hills are east of Qen."

He replied in his same even-tempered tone. "What makes you think we're going to the Iron Hills?"

"It makes sense that Monarchists would be going to help their brethren in the battle against Liberationist troops. The hills are riddled with mines where people can hide. Rumor says people are trapped there. Maybe you're out of oil and need Lamps to help guide people out. Folk are calling it the last stand of the Monarchists. But that fight was already lost."

"Was it?"

"My grandmother used to say Monarchist rebels are a twitching corpse that hasn't realized it's dead. Even if they were to win, which they can't, it's over for them. All members of the royal family were killed thirty years ago, everyone knows that. No royal child of the dragon lineage has been born in the years since."

"Yet your mother and father were hanged for distributing seditionist broadsheets."

Most of the time she could suppress the memory of being forced to stand in the back of a gaol wagon next to her grandmother and watch them hang: Mother's final defiant words to the sullen crowd and the sneering officials, Older Father dying quickly because the drop broke his neck, which was the most merciful thing that had happened that day. She breathed down the blast of grief and rage as she would carefully draw the energy out of a fire so it dampened and collapsed to coals.

But she could not resist a stab at the nearest target. "Is that what you think? That my mother and father were arrested and hanged for being Monarchist sympathizers?"

"Am I mistaken?"

"It's true they were hanged. It's true I hate the Liberationist Council for killing them. For imprisoning my grandmother. For taking me to Alabaster City to that pithole of an asylum to force me to serve them. For assigning me to that cursed establishment in Qen because the boss can afford my indenture fee. I get nothing but a hard bunk to sleep on and day-old bread and kitchen scraps for my dinner. So yes, I'll help you. There's an old trading road that stretches from the town of Zaren and across the Iron Hills north into the province where I'm from. If I go with you, then I'm ten days' walk from home."

The words left her out of breath from stark longing and a fear he would punish her for speaking her truth. She wiped her damp forehead with the back of a shaking hand.

He handed over a flask. "Take a drink."

She took a grateful draught of lukewarm cider. Its sweet alcoholic tang did make her feel better, although she was really getting tired. But to get home she had to walk. Such a long and lonely journey lay ahead of her.

As they headed out again, serenaded by the whisper of leaves rubbed by a breeze, the captain fell into step beside her.

"Dragon-born children still fall into this world, even if the August Protector and her council have proclaimed they've rid the land of the last of them."

"But the entire lineage was killed."

"That's not how it works. They aren't a lineage as you or I would know the names and alliances of our ancestors. Dragon-born children will always be born because there are rifts between the land and the aether. These rifts allow elementals to take root in our flesh as seeds take root in the soil."

"Elementals? Don't you mean demon-wraiths?"

"The Liberationists call them demons. They are properly called soul-wraiths."

"Soul-wraiths," she repeated. "Invi said that too. When I was little, elders were punished for using the word because it's Monarchist propaganda."

"No, Fellian. It is not propaganda. Soul-wraiths are so called because they are elemental wisps like an intangible shard of elemental spirit. Some people are born with them wrapped into their bones. No one knows why."

"Demons bind themselves to those who have enough evil in their hearts that it welcomes their embrace. Only the virtuous are free of their taint."

He sighed. "Soul-wraiths aren't demons. If you had ever fought or even seen an actual demon you would know the difference. Mage gifts have nothing to do with virtue. You are not demon-fettered, Fellian. None of us mages are, despite what you've been taught. As I said, some people are born with a soul-wraith bound into their bones as a slumbering elemental of earth, water, air, fire, or aether. Those who never feed and mold that wraith with training remain *roughs*. They retain an instinct for simple things but have no skill beyond that."

She thought of how Oran had heard Shey coming.

"Those who waken and shape the wraith can become mages. We are not and were never meant to become servants chained so others may profit from our skills. Our duty is to keep the land safe. The dragon-born are rare because they alone have all five elementals bound into them."

"Like a five-arrow quiver?"

"That's right." He nodded. "That's why they are called five-souled."

"That's what oracles are for, isn't it?"

"What do you mean?"

"The council uses oracles to sense the presence of elementals in an individual. Are you an oracle?"

"I am an aether mage but not an oracle. The Liberationist Council keeps all oracles locked up in the old monarch's tower in Alabaster City except when they are needed at census time to discover mages, like you."

She'd been too stunned in the wake of her parents' death to recall anything about the oracle who had identified her as a fire rough that terrible day. But she could still feel the grip of their cold fingers around her left wrist. "I wasn't taken at a census. What I mean is that if oracles can find five-souled babies, it makes sense the council would keep oracles under their control."

A quicksilver glimpse of dark emotion twisted through his dour expression. He said nothing. Maybe he was too angry to speak, but she wondered if the harsh set of his face was a remembered sorrow, a strike to the heart.

When he finally met her gaze she flinched at what she read there. "It would be wiser for you to ask what becomes of five-souled children when the Liberationists find them, even the smallest and most helpless. I think you already know."

They are monsters, and they must die.

"Helpless infants and innocent children, Fellian. Not

unlike you, when your parents were arrested and you were taken away."

"I was fourteen. Not helpless."

"Helpless to stop the authorities from hanging your parents."

"Yes, Captain. I understand the point you are making. Can we end this discussion?"

"Of course. You need to learn our signals. I'll start with the basic four: All Clear, Caution, which means to hold in place, Form Up, which means to form up on me, and Immediate Danger. There's a whistle for each, and a hand sign for when we need to communicate in silence."

They continued on the straight track. He was a patient teacher, running her through the sequence with no sign of exasperation when she didn't catch on right away and giving her long breaks. They never stopped walking, moving at a constant pace as the mid-morning sun rose toward zenith.

Haolu strode with head half cocked down like she was ready to bull her way through any obstacle. Invi walked with a smile, looking around at the trees and sky as if continually astounded by the world's beauty. As for Shey, he was incredibly skilled, and he didn't seem to tire as he opened one Eye after the next. How annoying was it that her gaze kept straying to admire his handsome cheekbones and lustrous eyes? Yet whenever they passed a flowering peony shrub that had taken advantage of the open track to grab a bit of sunlight, his mouth would tighten as a harsh misery crept across his expression. He would only relax again when the dusky pink flowers fell out of sight.

Everyone had their secrets, not just her.

"There it is," said the captain.

Ahead, the cart track reached a crossroads surrounded and sheltered by forest. A slender pillar stood at the center of the two intersecting tracks, its wood polished to a golden sheen as if an unknown attendant cared for it regularly. A bouquet of flowers and a cup of water had been laid as an offering at the pillar's base. For the first time she could see steep hills rising above the tree line and, almost floating against the hazy blue of the peerless sky, the peaks of mountains. They were entering the rugged northern regions of the country, closer to home.

A piece of blue detached itself from the sky. A bird plummeted from on high as if it had been waiting for them to appear. It opened blue wings and landed neatly atop the pillar. The captain extended his right arm, and the bird fluttered down to perch there. It had a fierce gaze, a toothy beak, and three legs.

Shey, Haolu, and Invi all took a step away from the bird. The captain slipped a message from a tiny tube fastened to the bird's middle leg. It flapped back up to the top of the pillar. He unrolled a tiny scroll, then blinked, frowning, and held it out at arm's length as he squinted.

"Too small to read," he muttered in a tone of disgust.

"So you're not perfect after all," said Shey with a grin

that could probably melt rust off bitter old iron. "Allow me."

With a flourish he plucked the tiny scroll from the captain's hands and perused it, eyebrows and lips raised charmingly.

His eyebrows dropped. His mouth flattened.

"What's wrong?" demanded Haolu.

When Shey didn't answer, as if he'd lost the power of speech, Fellian snatched the scroll out of his hand and read it aloud to the others.

"The oracles have spoken. We have confirmation by messenger pigeon. An earthquake in Flourishing Rose Province has leveled the town of Koryu."

Invi gasped, hand pressed to chest.

Haolu said, "Flourishing Rose Province? I've never heard of that place."

"Flourishing Rose Province is the name Jasper Province used to have, when the monarchy ruled," she said to Haolu. "The Liberationists changed the name so people like you and me would grow up not knowing the old name. It made them happy to do it because they thought they were striking a blow against the monarchy. But in the elder days it was the people who gave provinces and towns their names, because they were the ones who lived there and needed a name to call their homes by."

Staring at Fellian with a look of ridiculous surprise, Shey said, "I didn't know a farmer's daughter like you could read. They don't teach reading at the asylums. Can you write too?"

"What makes you think all my parents did was *distribute* seditious material that some wiser and more superior soul wrote for them?" she snapped.

She broke off because no one was looking at her. They were looking at the captain. As if felled by a stunning blow, he sank to one knee and shut his eyes, his jaw held rigid as if he had to clamp it down to stop himself from shouting, or weeping. She didn't know him and thus couldn't be sure. But he was the key to something momentous she didn't understand. Watching him, Invi pressed hand over heart. Shey bowed his head.

A strange anticipatory stillness settled onto them, movement held in check. The three-legged bird atop the pillar stiffened. Had it turned to stone? That's what was said in the old tales of the dragon monarchs, whose messengers bided in the poisonous storms of demonland until they were called into this world.

"This changes everything," said the captain in a hoarse voice. He rose. His stern expression did not look so different in feature and yet he stood even straighter, and with an even nobler cast of chin, as the poets would say. "We go south, to Koryu."

South and west, and thus about as far from home as Fellian could possibly get. She opened her mouth to object but Haolu leaped in before her.

"To Koryu? You told me we were urgently needed in the Iron Hills to rescue survivors in the mines."

"This must take precedence."

"What do you expect to find besides death and misery?" Fellian asked.

The captain turned to her. "Any time you hear of a remarkable earthquake or fire or flood or storm, that is the sign."

"The sign of what?"

"That a five-souled baby has been born in the region where the disaster occurred. We must reach Koryu before the August Protector does. I assure you she has also received this news and is already on her way to kill the child."

They walked the rest of the day at a brutal pace along a ribbon road. Shey opened one Eye after the next, never flagging or complaining. In the late afternoon the captain shifted them off the ribbon road and onto a cart track that wound through hills. They crested a rise to find a vast valley sprawled beyond. The steep hillside had shattered in the quake and peeled off. The remains of an avalanche piled up at the base of the slope. Uprooted trees stuck out of the rubble at crazy angles. In the distance fires burned, ash a spiteful flavor on the wind.

A tremor shook the earth. Shey stumbled and went down on one knee. The ever-dogged Haolu grasped his arm to help him up.

Invi said, "We'll hide in the trees to catch our breath."

"We must go on," the captain replied.

"Give them a chance to rest, my lord." Invi's usually cheerful voice took an edge. "Fellian, over there under the quickbeam is a good place for a nap."

Fellian dragged herself over, grateful to flop down on a blanket beneath the tree's scarlet berries. Her limbs weighed so heavily she was sure she could not rise even if they were attacked. Shey fell asleep at once while Haolu walked into the forest to do her business. Invi and the captain remained standing at the overlook, their voices floating on the air like those of actors heard from beyond a theater wall by people who haven't a coin for admission.

"They don't possess Haolu's stamina. Nor your stubbornness."

"Any delay will be fatal."

"Shey brought us thirty days' ordinary journey in a long afternoon's walk, my lord. You will break him if you keep pushing."

"We are made to be broken in the monarch's service."

"You and I are so made. We spoke the covenant. These young ones did not."

"Shey's mother did."

"She knew what she was walking into and accepted its cost. He does what he does for love of her."

"He acts out of honor and duty, as all of us must."

"Of course. But the two girls did not ask for this. The work you need Fellian for does not expose her to a sword to the gut with a public hanging afterward to finish her off."

"I promise you, Invi, on my soul and on my honor, I will not force the girls to risk more than what they are willing to take on."

"You need a five-arrow quiver to find the child. What if one refuses to go farther?"

"I will not force them. There are slower means to find the child, if it comes to that. But I believe they will both choose the honorable path."

"How your noble brow remains unclouded never fails to astonish me. You must allow the young ones to rest before we descend into the valley or we will not be able to rescue anyone, least of all ourselves. Sit down while I boil millet. If you can't sleep, then let us discuss how the encounter might go. Most likely. Most advantageous. Most lethal. To start with, we might reach the baby before *she* gets here. But if we enter the city after she arrives . . ."

5

Fellian started awake some time later. The nutty smell of cooked millet made her stomach growl. The worst edge of exhaustion had cleared although her muscles ached keenly as she clambered to her feet. Dusk cast a deepening blue haze over the sky, murky with ash and smoke.

"No, no, I'm fine," Shey was saying peevishly to Invi. He sat slumped by the steaming kettle, a spoon in hand.

She limped over, a blister rubbing painfully on her right heel. Crouching beside the kettle she waited for Invi's nod, then dug in. Haolu had gathered greens and bruise-berries to add flavor.

When her first hunger was sated, Fellian asked, "I know about Air Adepts because every once in a while one would be brought in to track down a servant mage who tried to run away. But they were the only Adepts we ever saw or heard talk of. What special skill does a Water Adept have?"

"What do they teach water mages at the asylum?" Invi asked. "I really do not know."

"You didn't attend one?"

"There were no asylums under the monarchy. Mages lived in respected guild halls."

"Oh. Well, they teach them how to heat water for kitchens and baths. And a water mage can test if water—or a travel token—is pure or tainted."

"That's all?"

"What else would there be? Fire to make light. Safe water for drinking and cooking. Air moves travelers. Earth trains and calms animals and gives soldiers strength for a long campaign. Aether senses illness. Mages must be taught to suppress their demon-infested cravings for power and corruption by being trained to serve, for the good of all."

Invi quivered with a frown so severe it could have chastened the air. "Outrageous! To teach you to hate yourselves. And then stunt you with ignorance. Sense illness, indeed!" The water mage snorted, then glanced toward the captain.

He stood in the growing shadows, staring toward the distant fire with its constantly shifting patterns. A gleam like a hint of mist rose off him. In daylight Fellian wasn't sure she'd have been able to see it. Not even the mages who taught at the asylum had been touched with so much elemental potency that it leaked from them.

"He's got to be an oracle," she whispered to Invi, for she could think of nothing else so powerful.

"He isn't an oracle," said Shey. "He's a path breaker."

"What's a path breaker?"

"Invi's right," Shey replied in a tone of haughty condescension. "It's outrageous you are only taught the basic level of magic and never allowed to study higher levels."

"As if you would know!" Fellian snapped. "You didn't live in an asylum!"

"People are born as Adepts," Haolu said in her stubborn

way. "Their demons are more potent than those fettered in roughs."

"It's not true," said Shey. "Any untutored mage has potentiality. That's why they're called rough. Rough as in raw, waiting to be shaped and trained. You're kept ignorant on purpose so you'll be content with servitude."

"What makes you think we're content?" Fellian demanded, thinking of how desperately Oran tried to hide his air gift. "Or stupid?"

"Enough!" The captain walked over to them. "If you three are energetic enough to bicker, you are energetic enough to march. Shey, you'll take point. Haolu second. Fellian in the middle with Invi next."

"How can you find a baby in such chaos if you're not an oracle?" Fellian demanded.

His gaze shifted to her. The thin ring of gleaming silver surrounding his pupils had a delicacy at odds with his grim expression. "I can find the child."

"What if I don't want to risk whatever we're going to do here? It's reckless."

His wry twist of lips surprised her. "I admire your plain speaking, Fellian. You can leave us now, if that is your wish. The work I need you for in the Iron Hills is a different sort of task than this one"—he glanced at Invi and then back to her—"and less immediately dangerous. Haolu, you may also go, if you wish."

"I'm with you, Captain," said Haolu stoutly.

Fellian said, "What about the travel token and money?"

Shey looked at her, disappointment in the tilt of his head. She felt a pang, wishing for him to have a good opinion of her. But it was ridiculous to be swayed by an attractive face, one out of her reach. She already knew the uselessness of that particular dream.

The captain said, "Invi, leave the travel license and the money for Fellian."

Invi blew a puff of air, then took a pouch of coins from the backpack and set it on the ground. They headed out, picking their way down the unstable slope before the daylight faded.

Fellian grabbed up the token and tucked it into an inner pocket of her soldier's coat. The pouch she stuck into the pack they'd given her. With that and the soldier's kit—weapon, knife, blanket, soap, comb, change of clothes, and a length of rope—to sustain her, she might have a chance to get home. Yet what if they really could save the baby? Grandmother would say it was wrong to turn away from those in need. If you weren't willing to risk your own comfort, or even your life, for what you believed in, then you didn't really believe in it.

She reached into a pocket and brushed the stub of charcoal, thinking of Nish and poor Karry who'd been transferred and frightened Oran who was so desperate to relearn his letters. She knew what her parents and grandmother would choose, and had chosen. So must she choose likewise.

She hurried after the others, coming up beside the

captain. "If we find this baby, we'll go to the Iron Hills afterward?"

"Yes, we will. There are people there awaiting us, who need a Lamp to guide them to safety. I will not abandon them."

"I overheard Invi say you need a five-arrow quiver to find the child. Why are you willing to let me go?"

"You're not required to put yourself in danger for a cause you have not pledged yourself to."

"You don't seem surprised I've come after you."

"Alone, you'll face a months-long, solitary, vulnerable overland trek to the Iron Hills. If you can even find the way and aren't assaulted or recaptured. You're safer with us."

"Really?"

"In a manner of speaking," he said with a smile, as if he had rediscovered the ability to laugh at himself.

Older Father had often smiled like that, droll and never mean. She missed him so much that the pain in her chest, the wrenching sense of dislocation and loss, could not ease.

The captain added, "From what I've learned of you in this short time, you would want your parents to be proud of the choices you make."

Moisture stung in her eyes. "Very well. I'll accompany you."

The main road through Korsuval, the valley of Kor, was choked with refugees who blundered forward through the growing darkness, desperate to escape the destruction. Many had wrapped cloth around their faces to protect against smoke, dust, and ashy grit, making them look like the mouthless demons of the old tales who were said to smother hapless victims in their sleep with a deadly kiss. Not that she had ever seen a mouthless demon for herself.

Because it was dark Shey could not open any Eyes, so it took half the night to trudge across the valley. Aftershocks trembled at intervals. Every time the earth shook, shouts and cries pierced above the low rumble. Villages stood crookedly, roofs fallen in. Village folk clutched scythes and axes, clustering around grain storehouses that had been wrenched off their pilings. Houses could be more easily replaced than these precious reserves. When these humble folk caught a glimpse of five people kitted out in soldiers' gear within the light of Fellian's pale Lamp, they called out.

"We need help here. Can you help us?"

The captain's reply was always the same. "We are being sent by order of the August Protector to guard the council treasury in Koryu."

"Clever," said Fellian as they left yet another group of frightened villagers behind amid the relentless flow of refugees out of the city. "They'll be angry the August Protector protects the council's riches over the people she claims to be saving with her revolution."

"If truth reveals the dishonest heart of the Liberationists, then so be it."

"The monarchy was rich too. Far richer than the farmers and laborers it ruled."

No anger sharpened his expression, only the weary resignation of bad news accepted long ago. "It's true that in the days of my parents and grandparents the monarchy had become corrupted by greed. Selfishness ruled the court. But the last queen was different."

"Was she?"

"You did not know her. I did. She was not much older than I was at the time. We were going to restore integrity to the court. As the court went, the realm would follow. Our cause was just."

The tight lines around his eyes softened. Something vulnerable and optimistic peeked out, a glimpse of a hopeful young man who'd gotten left behind, stranded amid the wrack and ruin of history. The sense they were walking into a maelstrom made Fellian bold.

"Were you in love with her?"

He missed a step, caught himself, then shook his head. "Enough," he muttered to himself.

"You were in love with the queen!" she cried, struck by a story perfect for a tragic ballad. "Did she love you back?"

"The queen? Of course I wasn't in love with the queen. I

served her with my whole heart and my untarnished honor. I was at the battle when she fell."

"Was she really killed by a humble ditchdigger?"

His curt laugh cut like a sword. "That story. Of course not. She was killed by treachery, by one of her trusted advisors and closest friends. To my shame I did not see it coming even though I had been warned. But I didn't listen. I could not believe someone I thought I knew so well would betray us for such mercenary reasons. So I lost what was most precious to me."

"Your belief in honor?"

"Honor never dies, even when traitors stab it in the back."

"Then what did you lose?"

He set his jaw, clamping down on any further words.

Invi looked back and, with the wave of a hand, beckoned. "Up by me, Felli. We're almost there."

Fellian picked up her pace. As she came up alongside the Water Adept she said in a low voice, "Did you ever meet the last queen?"

"Leave it be. We'll need all our wits to manage what lies ahead."

What lay ahead was a rage of fire and a pall of smoke, and maybe that was apt enough, as Older Father would have said since he loved to quote poets. Her eyes watered in the hot wind streaming off the city. The air got so thick with ash that she tied a handkerchief over her nose and mouth. Passing folk called out to ask if they had news of any haven to camp for the night. Someplace close by, for the exhausted children, frail elders, and suffering injured.

"Keep moving," Invi replied to each questioner. "It's safer on open ground."

The gates in the outer palisade stood wide open. Folk pushing carts out of the city choked the road.

Shey muttered, "I wonder how many of those people are householders saving what they can and how many are looters stealing the easy pickings."

Invi gave him a disapproving look, then addressed the captain. "You're sure we need to look in the town, not in the outlying villages?"

"The oracle named the town, not the valley, so we search the town. We'll need to find the Blessing House."

Invi intercepted a group that included a baby. "Comrades, your help if you please. We have orders to help evacuate newborns. Can you direct us to the Blessing House?"

By the way some in the group shifted impatiently, leaning like plants swayed by an outgoing wind, she guessed they were desperate to move on but afraid to insult a soldier by not helping. Invi asked a few more questions, then let them go.

"Good fortune for us, Captain. The Blessing House is close to the inner gate so folk from the outlying villages can easily come here for their lying in."

"Easily come to be marked into the council's census ledgers, you mean," muttered Shey.

"Move," said the captain. "We won't be ahead of the August Protector for long."

"If we even got here before her." Invi licked a finger and held it up to test the wind, as if the wind could give answers. But surely that was Shey's magic, not Invi's.

Like sticks jostling against an outgoing tide they pushed their way in past the gates. They walked through outlying districts with tanning yards and refuse heaps, humble bloomeries like cracked brick beehives surrounded by tumbled stacks of charcoal. The flow of people slackened. Some had hunkered down amid the work yards, hoping open spaces would protect them or perhaps to guard their livelihoods, but on the whole fewer were emerging from the inner town.

A violently bright fire burned in the distance where a blast furnace outside the walls had been set ablaze. This monstrous blaze was spewing out much of the smoke. It was this conflagration they'd seen from the hillside.

Koryu's high inner walls loomed into view like a blot of cold menace. Fellian was shocked to see an entire section of wall sheared off, rubble from its collapse strewn in heaps and ridges around a big gap. The inner gates stood open. They marched in past the main gatehouse, no soldiers in sight, no one to ask for travel tokens. The entry plaza with its five intersecting streets was eerily empty of life. A broken cart listed to one side. A bolt of cloth spilled open over its edge, the fabric fluttering as wind caught in its folds.

Other bits and pieces of shattered lives littered the plaza: a spindle, an indoor slipper stained with an unsightly blot that might have been blood or feces, a child's painted ball. Fellian scooped up a leather bottle with a broken strap. It sloshed with liquid. When Invi paused to get bearings, Fellian tied a knot in the strap and slung the bottle over her shoulder.

"This way." Invi led them to the second rightmost street.

This wide thoroughfare ran past abandoned shops before opening into a narrow plaza lined by administrative buildings. Their main entrances were recently painted with the names of government ministries: Tithing House, Responsibility House, Census House, Blessing House. Cracks had shot through the facades. All of the buildings had broken windows and collapsed awnings.

A tremor rumbled beneath their feet, punctuated by more crashing as roof tiles spilled onto the ground some ways down the street. Fellian jumped, cringing as she waited for the world to crash down on them.

Haolu touched her on the arm and said in a low voice, "This ground is stable. These buildings won't collapse."

"How do you know?" Fellian whispered.

"The captain taught me earth mages have a gift for finding solid ground. No one told me that at the asylum, did they? I think they really were lying to us about our gifts. But why wouldn't they want us to know?"

Fellian pressed a fist to her lips as if to stem the anger

boiling inside. "To keep us beneath them," she said into her hand.

"What?"

"Inside," said the captain.

They picked their way up the cracked steps of Blessing House and into an entry room lined with benches. In darkness they halted. Fellian saw the others as smears of variable heat. It was a skill she'd stumbled upon and secretly honed. She'd thought herself alone in this skill, a scout venturing into forbidden territory, but now she wondered what skills a Fire Adept could master.

"I can't smell anything but smoke," Shey whispered. "I'm not hearing signs of life except a cat on the stairs."

"Make a Lamp," said the captain.

Fellian shaped a small Lamp. Light revealed words painted onto the wall in red like blood: *Jojen Lives*. The captain caught in a sharp breath. Invi glanced at him but he shook his head to fend off Fellian's attention.

He headed into the back. Fellian set the Lamp floating at his shoulder. There was not much to see as they worked their way through the building. The main corridor had doors onto four wards. When she nudged her Lamp inside each ward, the light revealed a long chamber laid out with sixteen cots paired with woven wicker cradles. One ward was stripped bare, unused, but many of the cots in the other wards bore empty cradles set next to cots whose rumpled blankets suggested recent occupants.

"I don't like the look of this," said Invi. "Where are the infants and their parents?"

The captain nodded grimly. "You think the August Protector is already here."

Fellian's gaze caught on a shape half hidden behind an overturned cot in the far corner of the last ward, the heat of its life cooling fast. Her gasp brought the captain's head around.

"What is it?"

"There's a body over there. Recently dead."

His gaze stayed stuck on her for what felt like one breath too long. Then he went to investigate, kneeling behind the cot.

When he returned he said, "A farmer by his clothing. His throat was cut. He had this clutched in his hand."

The knit cap, sized to fit a baby, looked incongruous in the captain's callused, weathered hands. Shey took the cap from him, held it to his nose, then went to sniff around the corpse as a dog might.

He returned with a frown. "Nothing but his blood and his scent. If the cap was for a baby, it never wore it before he was killed." With a sigh he tucked the cap into a pocket.

The captain and Invi consulted in whispers, then led the group out the back of the building into a spacious courtyard with benches. No one asked her to search the courtyard for hidden bodies but she gave a long look around and was glad to see none.

The walls had cracked, bricks fallen in heaps. The big

back gate had been knocked ajar. Beside the gate stood a bricked-up five-arrow alcove, its lintel carving effaced. She wondered if eventually the empty alcoves on Qen's streets would be bricked up and defaced as well, one by one until they were all gone as if they had never existed. When the elders died, and their children after them, all memory of the old ways would die with them.

Shey stood with his head cocked to one side. "Deserted for as far as I can hear. But my hearing isn't as keen as most Adepts'. Isn't it most likely the families who were here have fled?"

The captain said to Invi, "We'll have to risk it."

"We'll probably end up walking into a trap."

"Probably." The captain looked neither excited nor fearful at the prospect of walking into a trap. Probably he had walked into, and escaped, a lot of traps in his life.

Fellian said, "Risk what?"

"Hush," said Invi.

The captain said, "Take position equidistant around me, in this order: fire, air, earth, water. Fellian, douse the Lamp."

They moved into position, standing like compass points with the captain at the center. Fellian pulled her Lamp's fire inside herself. At once, they were drenched in darkness except for the reddish-orange glow of flames to the west.

"Haolu and Fellian, you are about to learn one of the reasons five-arrow quivers are outlawed."

She had no idea what to expect.

A gleaming aetherical spool of wire-fine silver rose as if from out of his head. It spun like a shining horizontal wheel around the circumference of the circle the five of them made. A tickling sensation stirred in her chest.

Raising both hands, he tilted the Wheel without actually touching it, lowering it from above his head to a hand's breadth off the ground. When it began to roll, unspooling, he followed the silvery trail it made, for once taking the lead.

In silence except for the scuff of their feet they set after him, Fellian first, followed by Shey and Haolu, with Invi taking the rearguard. The streets were uneasily quiet and utterly deserted.

"You'd think there'd be more people searching for survivors or sheltering in the streets outside their homes to protect their belongings," Fellian muttered.

"Another reason it's likely the August Protector's troops have taken control," said Invi. "She keeps Air Adepts near her at all times, so no more talking."

A cat's forlorn meow pierced the air. Another aftershock rumbled, setting Fellian's heart beating hard. A low steady *thump thump thump* pounded in the far distance which she at last recognized as the signature of a working furnace. Someone had gotten one going. Which meant someone was in charge.

Haolu grunted as they crossed out of the district surrounding the gateway into a neighborhood that had taken far more damage. For the first time Fellian saw a body trapped in rubble, recognizable to her vision in the darkness by telltale spots of fading heat as the corpse cooled. She shuddered. Had the person been alive but unconscious when they'd been left behind? She hoped they'd already been dead. Was it better to die buried under rubble or to have your throat cut, like the farmer left behind in the Blessing House?

They picked their way past debris made by fallen walls and clambered over cracks in the street where the ground had split and risen up. The journey was accomplished in darkness and silence except for the silver of the Wheel, whose gleam did not reach the captain's face although he followed right behind it. Fellian guided herself by the heat objects gave off. Haolu had a sense of the ground that helped her move confidently despite the night's gloom, while Shey could surely hear all manner of tiny clues as to what lay around him. How Invi at the rear managed, Fellian did not know, but now and again she could have sworn she heard the sound of running water.

She wanted to ask where they were going but she kept silent, as ordered. Her footsteps scuffed too loudly. Her breathing thundered in her ears. Surely if there were other Air Adepts in the town they could hear them coming.

But no shouts broke their silence. After shifting from street to street on a twisting route Fellian could never have retraced, they emerged into a straight lane bordered by a high, white wall. The Wheel crossed the lane rather than turning to right or left. Reaching the wall, it began to roll through a bricked-up and sloppily whitewashed archway. Before it could pass through the sealed-off gateway the captain closed his hand into a fist. The Wheel vanished.

Evidently bricks were no barrier to aether. She didn't know. At the asylum, aether mages lived in an isolated wing separated from the main compound by a latrines court-yard and a wall. She was always an early riser and had soon learned to avoid the schoolrooms when teachers might cor-ner her there alone. So she'd gotten in the habit of practic-ing magecraft at dawn in the latrines courtyard. For her whole first year a sequestered youth had often peeked over the wall as the sun rose, watching Fellian's Lamp-work in snatches and then ducking back down for fear of being caught. A face to dream about, to wish for what could never be. They'd spoken with their expressions since speech was forbidden. Until now, that youth had been the only aether mage Fellian had ever had any interaction with, as slight as their knowledge of each other had been: long looks and blushing smiles.

A lingering aetherical gleam shone from the captain's hand as he measured the seals on the gate. Great iron bands clamped it shut. Above the gatehouse rose four thick posts, shorn off, the stumps of a scaffolding that had once been a watchtower. He shook his head although Fellian wasn't sure if it was a message that they could not enter by this route or his disapproval that what had once been proud and noble was now ruined. Shey caught Fellian's eye and offered a quick smile. She couldn't help the heat that flushed her cheeks, but at least he wasn't able to see her blush.

The captain beckoned them onward past words scratched through whitewash: *Jojen Lives*. His lips pinched tight but he said nothing. Invi's gaze slid to the captain's back as if to measure his reaction in his posture.

They walked quite a distance to the corner which led onto a wider thoroughfare, a grand avenue running perpendicular to the lane. The captain gestured for Fellian to peer around the corner while the rest stayed out of sight.

She stuck out her head enough to get a look. The smoke-filled night and the promise of violence made everything sharp: the air in her lungs, a tingle in her hands, the way her mouth felt parched. The thoroughfare ran for farther than she could see along more of the compound's high wall. Lanterns burning with ordinary oil hung at intervals along the wall. A coat of whitewash imperfectly covered old decoration, visible as shadowy bumps and knobs that would once have been a painted relief. Now she understood where they were.

This wall had once surrounded a temple dedicated to the cattle-horned moon goddess and her five-clawed portal dedicated to the dragon said to be ancestor of all the monarchs and thus the divine protector of the realm. In the old days the wall would have included four open entrances, one midway along each length of wall.

On this side of the grounds, facing east, the original archway had been concealed by a gated portico. The entryway's roof was held up by wooden pillars carved as statues displaying the eight virtues of liberation: Humility, Obedience, Gratitude, Fortitude, Patience, Thrift, Restraint, and Industry. Every city, town, and even the smallest village had a Virtues Garden wherever there had once been a temple. It was the law.

A rebuilt gatehouse sat in the center of the portico, four pillars to each side, controlling movement in and out of the garden. This gatehouse still had its watchpost, a crude tower made of scaffolding enclosed by a railing that stuck up above the gatehouse like a spire. Seen in the light of lanterns hanging from the portico, the gatehouse and watchpost seemed untouched by the tremors, maybe because they were built of wood or because of old magework woven into them.

Two soldiers stood guard on the portico.

She slid back and raised two fingers. Pointing at Shey, the captain indicated an ear.

Shey listened. At length he whispered, voice scarcely louder than breath. "No talking from inside the gatehouse. People in the grounds. Too far away to know how many or where."

"They'll be at the portal," murmured the captain grimly. "That is where she'll do it."

"It's a trap," said Invi.

"Only if she knows we are here already."

"She knows someone will come."

"But not when. Move out."

He headed around the corner and at a confident walk toward the portico. The soldiers didn't call out; they saw more of their own kind. Fellian hung back as the others followed the captain. On an empty side street in a strange city so very far from home, a flock of doubts and demands weighed on her.

It would be easy to walk away into the night. She could join the ranks of refugees fleeing the city, difficult to track in the chaotic aftermath. But she kept thinking about a helpless newborn being torn from the arms of a loving parent and handed into the cruel embrace of the August Protector.

That is where she'll do it, he'd said. Kill the baby, and its parents too, for good measure. Hanging in the Virtues Garden was the punishment reserved for criminals convicted of violating the tenets of the liberation. But of course the Liberationists were the ones who defined and codified those tenets.

As Grandmother said, they choose their laws to secure their power.

The others reached the portico. It happened so fast Fellian barely registered it before it was over: a greeting to allay suspicion, the captain and Invi striking down the two guards with the speed and skill of accomplished soldiers, no alarm raised, no cries, just collapse. Were they dead? She shuddered and yet it hit her with a flash of memory: bodies dangling, Mother's purpling face and kicking legs, the snap of Older Father's neck.

KATE ELLIOTT

She closed her eyes to banish the vision. To calm the sweats. When she opened them again no one was on the portico. Panicking, she ran. The gate was cracked open. Within its long entry passage, a latticework shutter had been forced open into the guardhouse. The captain wrestled a body through the opening, then swung over and dropped inside out of sight.

They did not intend to come back this way. They did not believe they would escape this without a fight.

She worried at her lower lip. For an instant she yearned for the safety of her bunk in the stable, the weary round of work at the inn, Nish's companionable face. But safety was a lie. Nowhere was safe.

Surely the captain and Invi had a workable plan. They had the bleak but calculated determination of people who have survived many trials and narrow escapes.

Swinging a leg over the sill, she dropped to the floor. The captain's hand had stopped gleaming with aetherical silver, but she could see all four in the total dark by the patchy glow of their bodies. Where the two soldiers' bodies had gotten to she did not know. She worked her way past tables and benches to join the others by a closed door that must let onto the garden.

"Here's the plan," whispered the captain as if he'd been waiting for her. "Fellian, shape a Lamp for Invi to carry." As she molded a small globe of fire into an object that, from a distance, would resemble a physical lantern, he kept talking. "Haolu, hold the inner gate shut until we come.

Brace yourself as I taught you. Shey, stay in the guard-house."

"But—"

"If things go wrong, you, Fellian, and Haolu get out by whatever means necessary."

She held out the Lamp to Invi. "Use gloves to hold it by this handle, if you can. I've layered it as well as I can, so it shouldn't burn you, but it will feel hot."

"Skillful work," said Invi with a smile.

The praise made Fellian tremble, thinking of how her family had encouraged her always and how she'd not heard a single kind word since that terrible day.

The captain said, "Fellian, go up on the roof. Keep watch for the heat of bodies. Anyone moving."

Body heat. "What gave me away?"

"I'll explain later. You are looking for individuals hidden from Shey's hearing. You all know the signals. Go."

7

A metal spiral staircase wound tightly up through a musty loft before cutting through the roof to the spirelike watchpost. The watch platform had an overhanging roof and a sturdy railing.

Fellian lined herself up along one of the roof posts, hoping it would conceal her in case the August Protector kept a Fire Adept in her retinue. If seeing body heat was what a Fire Adept could do. Did that make her an Adept? She didn't feel like one.

Before she had a chance to scan the garden, a door into the gatehouse opened and the captain emerged, carrying the Lamp. She blinked in confusion. Had the plan changed already? Then a second figure slipped out the door and onto a side path that cut to the left.

People had distinct heat patterns. The individual sneaking off into the shadows was the captain, limned by a faint silvery aura. Wasn't he? Was she mistaken? She shifted her gaze back to her Lamp, to the captain's face caught within the glow. His clothing. His sword.

No, there was something off about the way he was walking, a hitch in the disciplined rhythm of a stride honed by a lifetime of long marches. The heat patterns flowed oddly too, as if they were porous, restless, shifting. It made no sense. Invi had taken the Lamp but this person did not have Invi's face or form. How was that possible?

With a shake she dragged herself back to the mission. Distractions would kill you.

The Virtues Garden had straight paths and perpendicular intersections, everything aligned, proportional, and fixed as purity and truth are fixed according to the Proclamation of Liberation. At the asylum they had been required to memorize liberation precepts as part of their training and beaten when they forgot. The scars on her back itched, as they often did when she had to remember. She began to reach back there, then clasped her hands together at her belly to stop herself from repeatedly reaching for what she could not ease.

Enough. She had escaped. Keep the mind in the present.

Old magic imbued the temple grounds, too strong for the Liberationists to remove. All the paths held a faint silvery gleam not unlike the captain's aetherical aura. The central path led straight to an open space at the center of the grounds. From up here she could see the obscured lines of the foundation stones of a square temple. To her vision the lines looked like supple, braided arrows of magic in all five auras, woven into the earth in such a way that they could not be dug out.

The temple had of course been torn down years ago and replaced with a plaza paved with brick. All that remained of the old temple was its inner shrine, known as the five-clawed portal, since even the Liberationists didn't dare demolish its walls and roof. Instead they built eight-sided pavilions around each squat, square shrine to obscure it. A raised porch surrounded the pavilion and its eight support pillars. The octagonal pavilion's eaves were high enough to serve as a gallows. You could hang eight people at a time.

The people whose breathing Shey had heard waited at the base of steps that led up to the porch. Fellian identified one adult seated, holding an infant, and three adults standing at a respectful distance. Were the seated ones a mother and child? Were the others protectors? Or captors?

The Lamp kept its stately approach. Fellian scanned the garden and found the captain moving fast in the shadows, circling to get around behind the group waiting at the center.

A hedge ran parallel to the central plaza's paved edge, on the same side as the steps. Its dense thicket of leaves and branches obscured a group of five individuals clustered behind it. But she could see their heat. They were waiting to ambush whoever walked into the plaza.

It was a trap.

What use was a signal in this darkness? She licked her lips, tried for a whistle, but got only a dry puff of air.

Shaking, rattled, she scrambled down the ladder. Shey had the door into the garden cracked open. As she came up he put out a hand and, with unerring accuracy, touched two fingers to her chin in warning.

"It's a trap," she hissed. "Five behind a hedge, opposite the steps."

"I'll warn the captain."

"He said you should stay here."

"Do you have a better idea?"

The question wrapped like a noose around her neck. She did not have a better idea. She had no idea. As she stood rooted, trying to get her thoughts to line up into a plan, he slipped out the door and onto the left-turning path.

Eight against three. She didn't count the person holding the baby, whose arms would be full. Eight against three was no good. She hurried past tables and benches, crawled out the window into the passage, and saw Haolu by the inner door, steady and stable.

"Felli?"

Fellian pressed in beside her to whisper in her ear. "Ambush. We can cut around behind and flush them out."

"The captain said—"

"Eight of them. Shey went."

Haolu's shoulders lifted and dropped. She grabbed Fellian's wrist and squeezed so hard that Fellian thought her bones would be crushed.

"Is this true?"

"Yes."

She released her. "Lead on."

Haolu set the big gate ajar just enough to slide through. Fellian pushed her to the path that turned to the right. She meant to follow but, as Haolu vanished into the dark, hesitated instead. The Lamp she'd formed was by now a distance away down the straight path, although the light had not yet reached the central plaza. The person carrying it paced with a methodical tread. The people waiting at the center knew someone was coming. The slower the Lamp moved, the more time the captain had to move into place. The more time Shey had to catch up to give warning. Three against five wasn't such bad odds if the five got ambushed because they were paying attention to something else.

As the child of farmers she'd learned to wield a rake, a shovel and spade, a pick, a hatchet, a knife, and a machete, but weapons and combat training had always been forbidden to farmers and villagers. At the asylum, desperation had forced her to figure out how to use Lamps to keep people away from her body. All explainable as accidents, of course. Sloppy seams could distort and allow the Lamp to swell. If not sealed properly, Lamps leaked a scalding heat. If formed carelessly, as a beginner might do, they could even explode.

The Lamp was a distraction. So Fellian would distract.

The more noise the better. She trotted down the long paved path, making no effort to approach quietly. As she came up behind, the person carrying the Lamp cast a swift glance backward. He had the captain's face, and yet somehow the expression wasn't stern and somber enough. With a flash, almost a jolt, she remembered the words the soldier at the watchtower had said: *Mages who could steal the face of another person.*

It had to be Invi.

She followed the Adept into the central plaza along a

pathway lined with old stone water troughs repurposed into lotus gardens. They halted about twenty paces from the pavilion. Fellian stayed three paces behind.

The Lamp cast a mellow light over the scene. Shades of dark honey gold washed onto shores of deep shadows cast by hedges and thick-canopied trees. Stone flower planters that reminded Fellian of repurposed feed troughs lined the hedges.

Three individuals stood on the pavement at the base of the stairs that led up to the forecourt of the sealed shrine. One was a silver-haired man with a shiny burn scar along his jaw and a triumphant, condescending sneer on his arrogant face. She knew his type, a Liberationist who preached the virtues of Thrift and Humility while he himself dressed in the most expensive clothing and ate the finest food. Next to him stood a woman no longer in the first flush of youth but not yet old. She wore ornate rings on every finger but the unadorned clothing of a laborer, draped by a black-and-gold sash worn by the distinguished individuals who had merited elevation to the Liberationist Council. It took Fellian a moment to realize the silver-haired man wore a council sash too, so cleverly worked into the cut and color of his jacket that it did not disturb his fashionable appearance.

Three steps behind the councilors stood a thin, hollow-cheeked young woman. She wore the drab uniform of a servant mage with an aether badge sewn to her jacket. Though she stood with chin up and feet rooted to the ground, her restless hands betrayed nervousness as she studied the false captain. Then her gaze touched Fellian's in the glow of the Lamp. Her lips parted with a jolt of surprised recognition.

Fellian's body locked up as if she'd been punched in the head but could not fall. She'd seen that face so many times: distinctive eyebrows that met across the bridge of the young woman's nose. A wormlike white scar that cut its slash just below her left eye. The only youth bold enough to peer over the tall fence separating the wing where the aether mages were kept sequestered from the other young mages.

Fellian had been so lonely that year, so bereft, mourning her parents' deaths and the wrenching dislocation of being torn from her home and brought such a terrible distance to the grim confines of the asylum. If at first she had spent time in the latrines courtyard shaping Lamps to get away from groping hands and crude whispers, soon she had made any and every excuse for each chance to smile at a person who, like her, desperately sought the slightest brush of contact with a sympathetic face.

A voice cut across her thoughts.

"I expected you, and indeed here you are." The tone was low, gravelly, assured.

The aether mage flinched. Her fear made Fellian flinch, as if the old connection had never broken. But the aether mage sharply looked away, as if in denial, and turned to stare toward the temple with a tautness of expression.

At the top of the steps a woman sat on a canvas folding stool, the kind used by peddlers and itinerant singers. She held the haft of a threshing flail in her left hand. A large bell hung from the eaves above her, its bell rope dangling within arm's reach. The woman's ramrod-straight posture, iron-gray hair cropped close to her head, and expression of grave concern made her instantly recognizable as the August Protector herself, the Champion of Virtues, Advocate for the Weak, and Defender of Justice. In her right arm she held a bundled infant.

"I assume you came for the child." She allowed the silence to extend as she waited for the false captain to reply.

Did Invi's magecraft extend to voice? If it didn't, what then?

Fellian stuck her hands behind her back and hastily began shaping a Lamp in a form of her own invention, a ball-shaped tangle of fiery spikes. It wasn't deadly but it surprised people enough to shake them. Or maybe she was the shaken one, seeing the girl again a freshly opened scar. Her fingers moved like lifeless sausages, clumsy as she spun fire out of her bones.

The August Protector's expression remained calm and her tone considerate. "I suppose it is difficult to justify. For who would wish such a monster to live that causes so much destruction? A monster woven out of threads made of demon souls. I've never understood the Monarchists. Perhaps you can explain."

A short cough came from behind the hedge. The three companions all twitched and glanced that way, betraying they knew people were hiding there. A stamping of feet drummed beyond the hedge. Leaves thrashed in an eddying pool of wind. A voice cried out, followed by the hedge splitting in a great crash. A body stumbled through as if propelled by a shove too powerful to resist. The push of an earth mage.

The two council members stared, immobilized by surprise.

The false captain's face and body shimmered as heat does above boiling water. An odd shift of temperature washed over the plaza as Invi flowed back into the face and form Fellian knew. Shaking off his stupor, the man lunged, sword raised, at the water mage. Fellian threw her barbed Lamp at him. By sheer luck it struck him in the face. He reeled back with a shout. Invi scrambled after, kicking him in the stomach so he doubled over, then pummeling him to the ground.

The other council member grabbed the aether mage and tugged the young woman in front of her as a human shield.

Haolu appeared out of the night dragging a limp soldier by an ankle. She slung the soldier on top of the one she'd flung through the hedge.

The captain paced into view beneath the aura of the two Lamps, the one on the ground and the one floating in the air. His sword remained sheathed but he held a knife wet with blood. His gaze met Invi's, who lifted a chin in acknowledgment.

No sign of Shey. Was he dead? Dread writhed in Fellian's belly. But when she took a step toward the hedge, meaning to find out if he had been injured or—hells forbid!—killed, the captain caught her eye and tilted his head toward Invi. The water mage was pressing the heel of a boot down harder on the back of the squirming man, who was trying to grab his fallen sword. Fellian ran over and picked it up. The point dipped, the weight out of proportion to her strength. A sword was useless to her without training, so she shoved it under the porch's overhang and began shaping another Lamp.

Above them, the August Protector sighed with an exaggerated lift and fall of her shoulders. She spoke as calmly as if no bloody fight had just taken place nor her people been defeated and likely killed.

"It is an abomination to steal the face of another, as this Water Adept has just done. Do you not agree, Lord Roake?"

Lord Roake?

Fellian's gaze flashed to the young aether mage, who stared wide-eyed and open-mouthed at the captain with an expression of utter shock.

The captain did not even react. Could he really be the most hated enemy of the council?

Of course he could.

How had she not suspected all along?

The August Protector went on. "Assuming this *is* you. It's been some time since we last met. I recall you being a younger, handsomer man. Well, perhaps not more handsome. You're certainly distinguished now. Your selfless devotion has given you a shine of nobility."

His eyelids fluttered, although Fellian couldn't tell if he

was amused or shoving away a painful memory. He said, "In how many speeches and pamphlets have you decried the very idea of the existence of nobility and claimed it was only a mirage, a fable?"

"Nobility is but a fable, a self-serving story. Your day is long over."

He walked to the base of the steps. "That being so, you may as well let me take the infant. If my day is long over, the child is no threat to your order."

The August Protector's smile was perilous. "It's true that by itself one infant is no threat. I can confine such a creature in the Tower of Judgment and feel confident that of itself it cannot shake the strength of the liberation. But you will know it lives there. You will seek a second, when another such monster is born, as one will be in time. With two such beasts at your disposal, you will drown this peaceful land in your selfish war for power. You will release demon storms upon the land and call it righteousness and necessity. You will burn up the virtues that sustain us and replace them with grasping greed and the rot of corruption. You are a traitor to the liberation, Lord Roake."

He glanced toward the man lying on the ground with Invi's boot on his back. "Certainly you know how to identify a traitor."

"I did what had to be done, what you and that barbarian refused to accept," said the prone man in a harsh voice, words half muffled by the way his face was pressed against the flagstones.

The captain addressed the August Protector. "I suppose Eirukar travels with you everywhere. I'm sure he hopes to further enrich himself from the golden dust of your footfalls across the land you have beaten into submission. To further strengthen himself with the iron and copper sweat of your hypocrisy as you crush the people you claim to liberate."

The other council member laughed, even as she still held a knife to the throat of the servant aether mage. "Well deserved!" she crowed. "Eirukar is nothing but a cowardly backstabber who switched sides when he realized his side was losing. So have I said from the first day he stole a dead Liberationist's jacket and pretended it was his own. He is a thief and a liar, not that anyone on the council listens to my warnings."

"Fuck off, you old swine," said Eirukar. "You never risked your life in battle. You twiddle your thumbs and your paramours while you tote up the account books in your personal favor."

Haolu whistled. "Hshh! Two ugly toads fighting."

The council member tightened her grip on the young aether mage, though it was Haolu she spat her ire at. "Demon-tainted spawn! How dare you criticize your betters?"

"You people overthrew the monarchy because you said no one is better than another!" When Haolu sucked in an angry breath, she seemed to grow larger. "Or was that a lie to get the power and riches for yourself?"

Fellian had an answer but also a powerful instinct to not draw attention to herself.

The August Protector rose with magnificent ease. "All are born with the same opportunity to cultivate the virtues. Not all choose to do so. That fault lies in themselves."

The aether mage—still in the council member's clutches—cast a frightened look toward the steps. The young woman was expecting something terrible to happen, and that expectation drew Fellian's attention.

Because of where she stood she had a view at an angle up the steps, which were flanked by a doubled pillar on each side. A lattice fence ran around the inside of the platform so no one could touch the walls of the shrine. In a blob of shadow between the pillars and the lattice lay crammed a large patch of blotchy, fading heat. Dying fires looked like this, flames sinking to embers, and embers fading to ash. It was a corpse, almost cold. But the body wasn't what had caught her eye.

Curled among dead limbs lay a blaze of life the size of a newborn baby. It was fiercely alive, almost painful to look at not because it was bright but because of a rainbow aura whose outlines throbbed in her eyes. Could the captain see it? He could not. His gift lay in touch, not vision. He needed the Wheel.

"I have had enough of this disgraceful theater." The August Protector grasped the bell rope.

The captain lunged toward the steps. The council-woman shoved the aether mage at Haolu and rushed the captain with such unexpected speed that he had to side-step to avoid her. He kicked the back of her knee as she passed, and she lost her balance and fell with a satisfying smack onto the brick. But her attack had delayed him long enough.

The bell rang loud and clear. In answer, the high chimes of a handbell and then multiple more rippled back in answer from farther and farther away.

"Sound is magic, don't you think?" the August Protector remarked. "An inert bell can call so many to me. I knew you would come, Lord Roake, so I lured you in. You're surrounded. Surrender to me, and I'll show mercy to the child."

He waited tensely at the foot of the steps. "Why would I trust you?"

"If not for your stubborn refusal to give up, the Monarchist cause would have died years ago. Recant, and I'll spare the child."

He said, "You must know I will never betray my people or the cause I have served all my life."

"You already have."

A knife flashed in the August Protector's hand. She slit the infant's tender throat with a single deep cut, almost severing its head. Hot blood coursed over the woman's hands, its heat throbbing in Fellian's stunned vision. Her body went cold, drenched with horror at the callous cruelty of the act.

The captain staggered as if he'd been struck. Invi

shouted a wordless protest. Haolu yelled a warning. But they didn't know.

Fellian leaped in one bound from the ground up to the platform, dodged behind the pillar, and grabbed the other baby off the cooling corpse. A dead woman, all she had time to register.

The August Protector cursed. She turned with knife raised and thrust. Fellian twisted to the right, turning her back to shelter the baby against her chest. The blade scored along her left shoulder, parting the stiff canvas of her uniform jacket. Pain seared across her skin. She lost control of the Lamp she'd been holding in reserve. Its half-formed glow drifted up past her head to pour light over the porch.

The captain was already up the steps. He grabbed the forearm of the August Protector, yanking her back with so much force that she stumbled into him. His hand closed on her bare wrist, dragging her to a stop before she could again stab Fellian. His grip was strong, tendons standing out. As close as lovers, Lord Roake and the August Protector stared at each other. Her contempt. His blazing fury. A breath of locked, frozen silence.

His eyelids flared and then narrowed. His lips parted not with speech but with an exhalation. Exaltation. So might a worshiper catch a glimpse of the ineffable. So might a student look when for the first time they truly understand how letters make words.

The August Protector tried to break out of his grasp but

he twisted her arm down until she grunted and was forced to kneel with a groan. He set his knife against her neck.

"What aura does the child have? What eyes?" he asked Fellian.

The infant stared up at her, limned by its rainbow aura. Instead of whites and irises its eyes whirled like the slow eddy of molten mercury.

"This is the one you came for," she said in stunned recognition even though she'd never seen such an infant before.

His gaze flashed past her to the hulking presence of the shrine beneath the gallows pavilion. He glanced over his shoulder toward the plaza. During the scuffle, Invi had lost control of Eirukar, who had scrambled out of reach and now stood by the hedge, panting, knife in hand, unwilling to abandon the August Protector but knowing he was outmatched. The councilwoman was shaking herself off, pushing up to hands and knees as her nose and mouth seeped blood down her chin.

Everyone heard the hammer of feet: soldiers coming at a run.

"We have what we need," Lord Roake said to Invi.

"You know what will happen," Invi said.

"I accept the responsibility. Haolu, break the shrine gate."

As Haolu ran forward, Lord Roake whistled a signal: *Form up on me now.* In answer, Shey burst onto the plaza from behind the hedge.

Eirukar cried, "Sheykar! What are you doing here?"

As Shey darted past him, Eirukar reached out to snag the young man's arm. "Stay out of their way. The soldiers are coming to rescue us."

Shey jerked to a halt, the man's touch like a bolt affixing him to the ground.

"Your son is a traitor!" spat the councilwoman. "He's with them, just as I warned the council."

"Shut up, you old cow."

"You're a cuckold, you pride-addled fool."

"Sheykar. Where is your mother? I left you at home to guard her."

Shey's father was a member of the Liberationist Council? It was too much to take in.

The lattice gate splintered with a crash as Haolu kicked through it. Fellian flinched and the infant gave a startled cry. Shey broke away from his father and raced for the steps. Invi brought the sword's hilt onto the head of the councilwoman, knocking her back to the ground. These acts were too late and too little. They were trapped. In another few breaths the August Protector's troops would race into the plaza and surround them.

Haolu kicked at the sealed doors once, twice. The third time the right side cracked and sagged inward. She braced both hands against it and with a shove broke it open.

Lord Roake called. "Fellian! Get inside!"

They'd be trapped inside a sealed building no larger than a sleeping chamber. Not even Lord Roake with Invi and Haolu could fight off an entire troop of the August Protector's picked guard. They would all die.

The captain's gaze touched hers. He did not fear. He was not shaken. He had survived this long because he knew what he was doing.

The August Protector shifted her chin enough to catch Fellian's eye. Her gaze had a strange and compelling luminosity, as if her virtuousness emanated from her soul. "This stubborn rebel can offer you nothing. Show your loyalty to the liberation. You will be given riches and respect. You will no longer be known as a distrusted servant mage. This I promise. You need only kill the accursed child whose veins are already clotted with corruption and poison."

Fellian made her choice, sucked it in like the smoke of a funeral pyre, stinging and final. There was no going back. She took four steps to the broken gate. Invi and Shey crowded up the steps, waiting for her to go inside with the infant. Lord Roake pressed his sword against the August Protector's throat, keeping her hostage as Eirukar hesitated, choosing to wait for the soldiers rather than attack alone.

The young aether mage cowered ten steps away from him, no one near her.

Fellian caught her eye and shouted: "Come with us!"

The young woman shook her head with helpless fear. Fellian knew that look. *There's no way out.* The girl did not speak aloud but it was as if Lord Roake heard her.

"That's what they tell you," he called to the girl. "That's

why they keep the shrines locked up. But I can unlock the five-clawed portal in the presence of a five-arrow quiver and one of the dragon-born. We have a way out. You can be free." Then: "Fellian! Go!"

The young mage would have to make her own choice. Fellian had made hers.

The instant she stepped over the threshold an uncanny night blanketed her. Its pressure made her bones ache and her eyes flood with tears. There should have been starlight or Lamplight eking through the broken gates, but from inside she saw no sign the outside existed. She heard nothing, felt no movement of air, saw only a deeper darkness that was also an absence of darkness and a surging whisper as of a distantly heard thunderous gale.

A body bumped hard into her. "Felli? Ugh, what is this?"

"Haolu?"

"Shape a Lamp so we can see."

Fellian wove a one-handed simple knot of a Lamp. As it kindled, its heat warmed her skin but no light shone. The darkness swallowed its magic although she could see the gleam of the infant's eyes like tiny windows onto a maelstrom.

"Ah! It burns!" cried Haolu as the still-invisible Lamp pressed against the earth mage's sleeve.

Fellian slipped the knot inside her jacket. Her boot kicked a stone plinth, but when she felt at it, whatever statue had once stood atop it was gone.

"Shey, are you here?" said Invi right at Fellian's ear, making her jump.

"Yes."

Lord Roake spoke out of the darkness in his usual tone. "Haolu, move the gate back into place. Barricade us in as best you can." Then he added, "Hold on to the clothing of one of the others and do not let go, no matter what happens, do you understand?"

"I understand," replied a soft, fearful voice. The aether mage had made her choice. Her hand groped at Fellian's back, found the belt, and gripped tight, as if she had at last found what she longed for.

"Give me the infant," said Lord Roake.

Fellian handed over the baby and yet when it was gone she shivered, as if something important had been torn from her.

A pale aura bled into existence; its misty light shaped a freestanding arch made of stone as pale as fog. A second arch set perpendicular across the first. Together they created four openings. Lord Roake stood at the center where the two arches crossed, with the infant tucked into his right arm. A grinding and several thunks made Fellian turn to look behind but she still could see nothing.

Haolu bumped up beside her, saying, "Done. Closed. But it won't hold long."

He said, "Form a circle of fire, air, earth, and water."

They spread out to make a circle of extended arms and clasped wrists around the aura. The archway wasn't really there, and yet it was obviously there. Invi's skin felt warm, Shey's cool, beneath Fellian's hands. The aether mage still clung to her belt, frightened breathing a pant at her back. The knot of her Lamp warmed her skin like a second heart pulsing. A rattling noise broke against the darkness as if from far away, although they had not taken more than ten steps into the interior. The soldiers would shift the doors and be upon them at any moment. Her back itched. With each twitch she expected to hear the aether mage's scream and after that feel a blade plunge into her own flesh.

The silver-wire aether Wheel spun into existence, floating above Lord Roake's head. He pulled it down and tilted it sideways until it hovered a hand's breadth above the floor, a disembodied wheel of light ready to roll.

With a swift slice of his knife, he nicked the baby's tender arm. Cut its skin open. The soft flesh parted.

Fellian gasped but no sound emerged from her dry lips. Fear punched deep into her belly. What if his promises were all a lie?

Shey's grip on her wrist tightened, maybe to hold her up but maybe just to hold her back from grabbing the baby and running.

Blood welled up its arm, a liquid so dark it seemed black. A drop fell onto the gleaming Wheel. A flare of light blinded her, but after she blinked she could see for the first time the interior of the shrine: a square, low-ceilinged space with four plinths and four doors.

The Wheel shaded from silver to a moon-white glamor. It rolled forward. Instead of rolling out from under the portal's conjoined arches it impossibly cut into the air itself, like a knife opening a wound, like Shey opening an Eye. The world fell open as if its invisible skin had been peeled away to reveal a place farther inside, a chamber inside a chamber even though there was no space for any such thing.

The Wheel vanished through the opening and began at once to unspool its ribbon of light into a realm of surging light and darkness as into the heart of an unearthly storm.

"We're going into demonland," said Haolu in a tone of disbelief that gave voice to Fellian's shocked silence. "The demons will eat us."

Behind Fellian, the aether mage whimpered but did not loosen her grasp.

Lord Roake said, "Wraiths cannot enter a person who already has a wraith in their bones. Do not fear what you see. Stay on the path I take no matter what. On this road I must lead, so Invi will take the rear. Haolu, you next to Invi. The soldiers may pursue us even into the realm between, so be ready."

Sheathing his knife and drawing his sword, and with the infant clasped against his body, he took a step onto the silver ribbon. A second step took him through the wound in the air, and he vanished.

Shey slid through as easily as he might step through an Eye of his own making, and he too was gone. A monstrous rattle thundered in the distance like boulders grinding shards to dust, a portent of doom. Hot rain sprayed out from the gap to spatter Fellian's face with the taste of hopelesness. She could not move. Could not go in. She could not. It was demonland.

"Move! Go!" Invi shoved her hard.

Thus propelled, Fellian's body hit what felt like an invisible wall with a tear in it that she had to squeeze through. The slit pressed around her, slippery and tight, as if to swallow her whole down a constricted gullet. Pressure popped in her ears as she was spat out.

She stood on a massive square pillar of black granite. Its flat top was the exact same dimensions as the foundation of the shrine. Below, the pillar's length disappeared into clouds of metallic feathers whose churning whirlpools hid the ground. Above, the heavens wore a sheen like the underside of blood-soaked ice. Freezing wind battered her with icy hail, succeeded by a bellows blast as from a furnace's maw thrown open.

Demon-wraiths writhed past, borne on powerful gusts. Here in this otherly world they appeared as benign clumps of pale filaments, like wispy roots. Yet for all they seemed insubstantial and frail, any living creature they touched would die.

Where was the captain?

Lightning crackled across the heavens as if through a vast net. The searing brightness revealed Lord Roake standing a stone's throw ahead on the ribbon path, which floated in the air like a bridge supported by unseen pillars. He was soaked to the skin from a downpour, although no rain touched her. He had halted where the ribbon path split into four strands. Was the splintering of the path his doing or the Wheel's unraveling? Each path wound a separate way into the turbulent landscape.

He stood with a booted foot on one of the middle branches, as if he hadn't made up his mind about which path to take. Instead of a baby, a tiny silvery-white dragon clung to his chest, wings furled and foreclaws gripping his shoulders to leave both of his arms free.

Shey moved cautiously forward on the ribbon path toward the captain, as if fearing he might tumble off. Fellian knew she had to follow but her boots weighed like lead, trapping her on the stability of the pillar.

The aether mage shoved past Fellian, her face twisted with fear. "I'd rather die in demonland than take another breath as their servant."

After pushing rudely past Shey, she ran to the captain, heedless of the violent sky above and the long drop to a surging ground below. Still Fellian could not make herself move. Behind, a shriek chased through the cleft that led back into the garden. The sound scalded the air, gusted past her in hot waves, as if cries of pain manifested in demonland as physical blasts of heat.

Invi squeezed through the wound, dragging a half-fallen Haolu. "Felli! Help me!"

Invi's voice jolted her into action. She grabbed Haolu's other arm and slung it over her shoulder. An earth mage weighed the same as any other person and yet there was a solidity to them, a sense that threads of rock and earth knit their sinews. But even an earth mage's flesh could not repel metal. A crossbow bolt stuck deep into Haolu's back. A froth of blood foamed up along the shaft. Yet still the earth mage set one foot after the next, face ashen.

By the time they reached the place where the ribbon path splintered, the others had moved on. The wind had blown the other three paths into a wild maze of intertwining trails, making it impossible to trace which path the captain had taken. But Fellian identified the fading heat of bootprints.

"This one."

"Good girl," said Invi.

They pushed against the gale with Haolu between them. A crossbow bolt tumbled past on the wind. Multicolored lights burst like fireworks overhead, showering the scene with sparks. Eight soldiers emerged onto the pillar out of the gash. Their faces were concealed behind the half masks used by the Liberationists' merciless Rectitude Corps. Three held crossbows, three had unsheathed swords, and the ones at the front and the rear carried bladed pole weapons. The August Protector herself appeared at the slit like a person peering past a curtain. She stared into the demonland with one hand gripping the threshing flail's haft and the other a rope that, tied around her waist, kept her anchored to the shrine.

A wraith spun toward her. The August Protector snapped out the flail to bat away the filaments but they caught in the chains. As if alive they slithered up the haft. Leaping the gap the wraith's roots reached for the woman's face. Yet when its probing tendrils touched her skin they recoiled and released. The wind blew them away. The August Protector shouted, words lost to the storm, then retreated back into the world they'd left behind.

"Stop staring! Move!" shouted Invi.

The lead soldier reached the split in the ribbon path. No fire mage, he made a judgment by eye, gauging the closeness of his prey. He plunged onto a path whose route had shifted so close to where they walked that Fellian was sure he was about to catch them. But the ribbon he walked on snapped outward, curling away with such speed that he stood a spear-thrust away one moment and the next became a distant figure struggling to remain upright. A bubble of black tar surged up from the ground. He lost his balance and fell. His scream ceased as the tar swallowed him.

The soldier behind him did not fall back. He examined the paths, waiting for the third, who, coming up, pointed to the one they had taken.

"That's a fire mage," said Fellian.

"Stop looking back!" Invi dragged the earth mage forward as Fellian scrambled along.

Haolu coughed. A foam of blood coated her lips. Wraiths twisting in the wind changed direction, filaments flicking back and forth like tongues tasting the air. A thread's tip brushed Fellian's cheek. A barbed hook like a thorn stabbed her, digging into her skin. She wanted to fling Haolu off, to leap, to run, anything to get away from the fatal touch. The captain's words flashed in her head: *Stay on the path.*

A second tendril cut like stinging ice up her cheek until the tip found a nostril and horribly slid inside. Ice lanced up into her sinuses. A shrill whine cut like a knife through her head until her eyes grew damp. A tear slipped down her cheek, and when it hit her mouth she tasted blood.

Demons devoured you from the inside out.

She shrieked, letting go of Haolu to try to grasp and pull on the tendrils but she couldn't get a grip on their slippery threads. Her right foot slid off the path, and she fell, body on the ribbon and legs dangling off over the gulf of air. Heat pressed upward in waves, promising a quick death in boiling tar if she jumped. The leather of her boot got hot, starting to char. Maybe it was better to leap than to die by being eaten from the bones out.

The knotted Lamp tucked into her jacket flared as with a splash of anger. From deep in her bones, from the weaving of her flesh, a spirit of fire raced to confront the intruder.

It burned until her sight went blue-white. The icy thread retreated. The wraith let go, and the wind tore it away.

Panting, crying, she hauled herself back on the path. Invi had dragged Haolu on, leaving her behind. Scrambling to her feet, Fellian looked back. Another shower of brilliant sparks lit the turbulent landscape.

A cluster of wraiths swept into the remaining soldiers. Tendrils fixed to their exposed skin. Yet the men kept coming, seemingly unaware as threads as insubstantial as smoke insinuated themselves through mouth and nose and eyes.

Fellian bolted after Invi. Coming up from behind she grasped Haolu. Labor steadied you when you had nothing else. She and Invi hastened as well as they could manage with the burden of Haolu and her ragged breathing and bloodied spittle. More and yet more wraiths swirled out of the sky, attracted by the blood, but the demon threads could gain no purchase on any of them, just as the captain had said.

Shey appeared out of a cloud of filaments so thick it made a curtain that blocked their view. He swept his arms back and forth like a flail. As the wraiths scattered, Fellian saw he was standing on a massive black granite pillar so exact in proportion to where they'd come through that she feared they had simply circled around. An open gash pulsed as a reverberant clangor sang through the portal: the sound of a ringing bell.

Lord Roake and the aether mage had already gone through.

Shey pushed Fellian forward so hard that her first thought was he meant to propel her to her death off the pillar. Instead she plunged through the gash. Its lips were rimmed as with sand, scraping her face and blinding her eyes. She slammed into stone. Winded, shuddering with pain, she bent over. Her jacket gaped, and the knotted Lamp tumbled onto a mosaic floor strangely free of dust and dirt.

She could see. She was in a square chamber exactly like the one they had entered in Koryu's Virtues Garden. One of the doors stood open to admit a cold breeze. A tender gleam of moonlight spilled across the floor to touch the glow of her Lamp. Four hulking figures surrounded her: each a statue, although it was too dim to make out what they depicted.

The portal oozed like a clotting cut trying to knit itself closed, as if the passage between this world and demonland was an injury in truth. As if the captain had sliced open a wound in and a wound out. As if the demonland was a vast intangible creature woven invisibly through the world but not visibly of it, a being of aether whose surface tension lapped the physical world of earth, air, fire, and water. Whether creature or realm, it was an ocean inimical to the life of the world. Lord Roake, Aether Adept and path breaker, had created a ribbon bridge across its wilderness to safety.

Or were they safe? Where were they now?

A strong light seared outward from the gash as a body

emerged. Shey dragged Haolu through. In their wake spilled clusters of wraiths. Misty tendrils spread into the air but when Fellian blinked they were gone. Had she seen them at all, or only imagined them?

Invi arrived, sword in hand. "Rectitude on our heels."

Lord Roake waited at the open door, sword in his left hand and infant tucked in his right arm. His gaze flicked over Haolu and the blood spume on her chin and chest.

"Shey, take the baby to the infirmary and give it into the keeping of Lady Ilfiantel, none other." He thrust the infant into Shey's arms. The Air Adept hurried out through the door. "Fellian, go with Haolu."

"She can't walk."

Several individuals in long tunics hurried in from outside to hoist Haolu between them and carry her out.

"Go with them," said the captain.

A cow bellowed.

A cow?

The sides of the cleft had, like the lips of a fresh wound, at last touched, but a pressure from the other side, the slash of a blade, hacked it open again. Men burst through, screaming as they lunged at the captain and Invi, death in their eyes and ghostly tendrils like root hairs sprouting from their bodies.

"Go!" shouted the captain.

Fellian sprang for the door and crossed the threshold onto a tidy porch. Behind, steel clashed, but when she looked back she could see only auras of body heat blurring and distorting in darkness. Her Lamp had gone out, and her body blocked the moonlight.

"Follow me!" Shey called from ahead. She pulled up at the top of a short set of stairs that led down into . . .

A cattle pen.

The shrine stood in the middle of a fenced-in livestock yard covered with sawdust and littered here and there with cow pats. A horned cow stood at the base of the steps, a bell dangling from its neck. It snorted, head dipping, as if daring the intruder—her—to come down off the porch. There were other cows—all horned—a herd slowly gathering to face the opening. From a corner of the large pen a massive bull loped over to see what was going on.

The young aether mage stood on the steps, clinging to the railing. She said, "We can't outrun a bull."

"Come, come," called the shadowy figures who had appeared so suddenly and between them carried an unconscious Haolu. They were already making their way through the waiting cows, who paid them no mind. "The cattle won't disturb you, child. Come with us."

The aether mage hurried at their heels, biting on a fist in her terror, but Fellian could not move, could only stare.

A pinkish glow lightened the gloom from the east, obscuring the moon. The air swirled as with wispy tassels blown from trees in spring. Ghostly clusters of wraiths had escaped from the aether realm. Beyond the fence lay a cow shed, a longhouse with a chimney, an orchard, and a garden, all surrounded by a high wall like that around a Virtues

Garden. The wall had four gates with a watchpost rising above each one. On the platform of each watchtower stood a round mirror like a silvery moon caught between two horns. People were up on the towers, turning the mirrors to flash inward across the livestock yard.

And beyond the wall? Maybe a village or a town, so many vulnerable people. The demon-wraiths would slide inside them and then . . . well, then they would warp painfully and horribly into demons.

The bull trotted up and planted itself to face the steps, pawing the ground and snorting in a cadence familiar to Fellian from childhood. A stirring as of wind rushed along her back. Invisible tendrils tickled her neck, slipped over her hair, swirled past in a drift of pungent, almost sickly sweetness. She could no longer see the wraiths, because they were not of this world. They gave off no heat as living creatures did, but the cattle tossed their horns as if catching threads, and dipped their heads to graze along the ground as if eating what they'd caught. The bull stomped and snorted, tail whipping to flail unseen wraiths to the dirt.

Lord Roake stepped up beside her, breathing hard. Blood spattered his clothes and dripped from his blade. "They're dead but they won't be down for long. Fellian, I told you to go with the others."

"This isn't a temple. This is a . . . a . . . livestock yard. Are the cows . . . eating the demon-wraiths?"

From inside Invi called, calmly, "They're stirring."

"Is the portal closed?" the captain called over his shoulder.

"Not yet. This will be a bad storm whose winds will reach all over the land."

"So be it. The sacrifice is necessary."

"The sacrifice of what?" Fellian said. "Of letting people be turned into demons? Killed by demons?"

"There are all manner of demons in the world, Fellian. Some are entirely human. Enough gawking. Go after the others."

She hadn't the courage to disobey that tone when he used it. He was sure of her obedience because he was the captain. Because he was more than the captain. He was Lord Roake.

Shey, the aether mage, and the strangers carrying Haolu had reached the fence. A woman opened a gate to let them through. She wore a drab tunic covered with a vest of sewn-together shells and carried a spear adorned like a flail with dangling braids of human hair. As soon as Shey and Fellian hurried out behind Haolu, the woman entered the pen. Another five people dressed like her emerged at a run from the longhouse and raced through the open gate in her wake. An old man hurried up to close the gate.

Fellian skirted the grazing cattle and the armed folk who moved among them running the flails along the ground as if to rake up any wraith debris.

The old man opened the gate. "Come along. We didn't expect his lordship to arrive by this path."

He directed Fellian toward an orchard of persimmon and walnut. She ran to catch up with the others.

The aether mage dropped back to walk beside her. "Do you remember me?" she said in a low, raspy voice, as if her throat was dry and she wasn't used to asking questions.

"Of course I remember you! You were the only good thing in all my time at the asylum."

"I remember you. I thought about you, after they took me away."

In a way Fellian was relieved she could not see the other woman's face. She tried out an answer, and then another one, but her tongue turned into a knot. Her silence lumbered like a third presence between them as they approached one of the compound's walls. A barracks was built against it, set with multiple doors and pierced by numerous chimneys.

A door stood open, and from this threshold an elderly woman wearing a gray scarf squinted at them. "Demon eaten?" she asked, indicating Haolu.

"Shot with a crossbow bolt," said Shey.

"In the lungs," added Fellian.

"To the left, then." She clapped her hands.

"What about the baby?" Fellian added.

The woman had already vanished back inside.

"I just want to see Haolu settled first," said Shey. "To see if . . ." He had a grim look about him, eyes bloodshot with exhaustion. "I'm the one who found Lulu. Who got her free from her indenture. I thought I was such a hero." He looked away, hiding his face. His shoulders heaved.

Fellian touched his arm. "You are."

In a voice trembling with intensity as he stared at her, he said, "Thank you."

A door to the left opened. Two women dressed as orderlies in knee-length aprons showed them into an infirmary room fitted with a wooden table and cabinets. The two who carried Haolu gently braced the unconscious young woman on her side on the table to avoid jostling the embedded bolt. A bubble rose, and popped, on her pale lips. She still lived.

Several more people arrived, carrying a brazier alight with coals and several buckets of water, and departed. The orderlies arranged medical instruments on a polished silver tray. The elderly woman returned with a box of ointments and herbs.

Fellian sank down onto a bench, looking to either side. "Where's the mage?"

"She didn't come in," said Shey.

"What if she runs?" She set feet under her, meaning to stand, but she just didn't have the strength.

"There's nowhere for her to go. We're high in the mountains. The only way in and out of here is through the mines, and you need magic for the passage. We need you."

"Oh," she said, not that his words made any sense.

He sighed, staring at Haolu's slack body. The baby nestled in perfect stillness in the crook of his arm. Had her eyes tricked her in the aether realm? Had it really transformed into a tiny dragon? Or had she just been seeing phantasms, for wasn't it said demons caused hallucinations? The uncanny eyes were open, and the baby had no white, no iris, no pupil, just a molten eerie quicksilver gaze. Even so, the infant was so small and helpless that Fellian couldn't think of it as a monster. It was just a baby being pursued by people who wanted to kill it.

Probably she should go look for the aether mage. She should go back to the livestock yard in case there was anything she could do to help the others. But her legs were lead weights. Her eyes slid closed, and she dozed off.

The sound of a latch clicking open jerked her awake.

A middle-aged woman with stern features entered through an interior door. A fish-and-lotus-flower-patterned silk scarf bound back her hair. She was tying a surgical apron over a linen gown too elegant to belong to a servant. At the table her practiced gaze and neat probe of Haolu's injury made a swift diagnosis.

"We must get the bolt out if we hope to save her. Everyone out but my orderlies." Her glance snagged on Shey. "Aren't you Peony's boy?"

Peony?

His cheeks darkened with a flush of shame.

"Hey!" said Fellian, angry on his behalf and her patience worn thin. "We have to deliver this baby to Lady Ilfiantel. It's important."

The old woman in the gray scarf rounded on Fellian. "You are not to speak to her ladyship in such a tone, girl!"

"Enough, Gifa!" snapped the fine-gowned woman, her

inflection on the word "enough" so like that of Lord Roake that Fellian wondered if they knew each other. "If there is a baby, and the portal, that means . . ."

"Yes," said Shey wearily.

The woman pressed fingers to her brow, shut her eyes as the orderlies stared as if they had just that moment noticed the infant in Shey's arms. Maybe they had. The baby had remained unnaturally silent, almost invisible, throughout the ordeal.

The woman lowered her hand. "We must accept what the goddess gifts to us," she muttered peevishly, then took hold of herself. "Gifa. Take the baby to the manor house. Give her into the keeping of Lady Mihetriel, none other. Double the guard on the compound. No, triple it."

Shey did not even open his mouth to protest this high-handed treatment, but Fellian jumped to her feet. "We were ordered to give the baby to Lady Ilfiantel, no one else."

"I am she. Do as I say, girl. Then get out before I slap you. I don't have time for your presumption."

Gifa said, "The sap-drinking dirt-shod drab likes of you must address her as 'my lady.'"

The words pummeled her with fresh savagery. She'd not heard the like since the asylum. In Qen she was an oddity, either ignored or treated as a fetish. Lady Ilfiantel had already turned away, any further discussion beneath her notice.

Shey said stoutly, "Fellian is the Lamp who will save the refugees. Gifa, do not scorn one who has risked so much to help us."

Fellian murmured, "It's all right, Shey."

"Lord Sheykar to you, even if you've bewitched him with those honey eyes," said Gifa with a huff of outraged dignity. "If you will, Lord Sheykar. The baby."

He handed the baby over and went outside, rubbing his eyes.

Fellian followed him into the bright sunlight. "You forgot to mention the cut on its arm."

"That's the least of our worries. It will heal."

"Are Monarchists all this rude?"

"Give it a rest, Felli!"

"Here I thought you meant to defend me, but you defend them instead. I should have known better."

"I'll leave you alone until you're in a calmer mood," he said in a tone perhaps meant to be kind but drenched with the condescension of one who has never truly had to back down. She was glad he walked away before she yelled at him. He headed back toward the pen. Just as she decided to follow, a moan quavered from the interior: Haolu woken by pain.

She sprang for the door. An orderly slammed it in her face. She flinched back as if she'd been kicked. The fear and the rejection were too much. She sank to the ground, panting as she tried to catch her breath. It was always people like Haolu who took the brunt.

"Are you hurt?" The aether mage appeared at her elbow, speaking in a voice so thin the air tore it almost to nothing. She knelt but did not touch Fellian, although she leaned toward her as a person suffering from cold leans toward heat. "I wanted to come in but . . . I don't like closed spaces."

Blood thundered in Fellian's ears and slowly ebbed. She raised her head to look at the face she'd smiled at so many times, the face that had smiled back like a gift. The aether mage was so scrawny she appeared childlike in many ways, but most likely she was older than Fellian. The census took roughs at age sixteen, saying they weren't trainable until that age. For two whole years Fellian had been youngest in her asylum. This frail person must be at least twenty.

"What's your name?" Fellian's voice rasped as harshly as if swallowed demon tendrils had scraped her throat raw.

She bit her lip, worrying at it. "They call me Ervia."

"Ervia is not your name?"

"No."

"Then what shall I call you?"

"It doesn't matter." With a nervous gesture she pressed a hand to her own cheek.

"It matters to me," said Fellian.

She kept her head bowed, looking up through her lashes, and braced her shoulders as if for courage. "They hit me when I told them Ervia is not my name."

"I'm not going to hit you, or let anyone hit you. But let's leave it for now, since it distresses you."

Ervia's smile was a glimmer of sunlight on a cloud-wracked day when you thought the rain would never break.

A flush heated Fellian's cheeks. "Do you remember the first time you looked over the wall?"

A bright blush painted Ervia's pallid skin. "It was early, just before dawn. I saw your face glowing in Lamplight. I'd never seen anyone who looks like you, and then you smiled at me—"

Shouts rattled the air. A scream. A stampede of cows.

Shey, somewhat down the path, started to run.

"Stay here," Fellian ordered, and she sprinted after him.

By the time she pounded past the longhouse and into view of the pen she was out of breath, fear thick in her throat. Nothing in her life had prepared her for the wild scene that met her eyes.

The captain, Invi, and the priests formed a semicircle, facing the open door into the shrine's interior. A creature stood poised on the steps. Mist eked off the body. It had been a soldier once. She could tell by the shreds of its uniform. Now it looked like a monstrous deformed spider trying to twist itself into being out of the flesh and armor of what had once been human. The torso split as a rib thrust out, extruding and growing to become another limb. The creature screamed; it was the scream Fellian had heard before. Was the man not dead but trapped inside the monster as it perverted his flesh and bone into a new body for itself?

A second demon nosed forward through the door, long of snout and bearing a feathery crest whose fronds were tipped with human eyes.

Shey leaned against the fence looking tired but strangely unworried. "See, one is already caught," he said as she ran up beside him.

The bell cow and the bull were trampling a third intruder, stirring the greasy remains into the dirt. The rest of the herd had scattered, eating through remnants of dying wraiths as if grazing on grass.

A hot sweet reek wafted on the air, nothing like the smell of blood or flesh. Bile rose in her throat. Questions raced through her mind but she did not know how to ask or how it would end.

A spearman darted forward to thrust at the spider-monster. Chains swinging from the spear's haft sliced through the demon's body as if it were mist, tearing it to shreds. It shrieked again, the sound so shrill Fellian pressed her hands over her ears, but flesh was no protector against a demon wail. The scream drilled down as if to burrow into her spine and corrupt her into a being who did not belong in this world. Her fire rose to meet it. She burned.

Wind spun furiously around Shey. The captain gleamed. Invi shimmered as if to flow out of one form into another before stabilizing back to the face and form Fellian knew.

The priests—for they must be the Children of the Moon Goddess, long since outlawed and persecuted by the Liberationists—stood stolidly as the spider-monster dissolved. Runnels like thickened cream oozed down the steps.

The long-snouted monster darted forward, bowling over the bold priest. With a splintered femur it stabbed the man in the gut. As the man went down, clutching his abdomen, the bull charged, caught the monster in its horns, and tossed it skyward. When the body hit the ground the bull trampled it until the substance of the thing was smeared as foam across dirt and sawdust.

The others grabbed the fallen priest and dragged him out of range. The captain and Invi ran up the steps to peer inside. When they came back out they shut the door. A latch thunked down. Fellian slumped forward, leaning against the fence.

Shey said, "Are you all right?"

She swallowed the sour taste in her throat. "Who is Peony?"

His parted lips, softened with concern, pinched tight. "What a thing to ask after everything we've gone through."

He walked over to open the gate for the priests. The wounded man was still conscious as his comrades carried him through, headed for the infirmary.

"Oof, thank the moon young Stubs didn't trample my balls, eh?" the man was saying in a wheezy voice, scratched with pain. His left hand was mangled and his nose broken. The stab wound was deep in his hip, near the bone, but no spouting blood or reek of guts bled from him. It had missed his vitals and struck muscle.

A cold wave of certainty swept her like an ill wind: *He'll live, and Haolu will die.*

The captain and Invi reached the gate as the bull swung its head around to glare. As Shey shut and secured the gate behind them the bull gave a final snort, satisfied that he had driven off all enemies. He was massive, solid, and comforting because he wasn't a demon, just an ordinary animal.

Invi used the back of a hand to wipe a bloody forehead but the gesture merely smeared the blood into patchy streaks. "Whew. That was messy. I wasn't sure you really would open a portal."

"I had no choice, not if we meant to save the infant. Shey?"

"The baby was taken to the manor house."

Lord Roake nodded.

"What happened to those three?" Fellian asked as, in the peaceful light of the rising sun, the herd grazed across the disintegrating remains of the misshapen soldiers.

"They had no protection against wraiths," said the captain.

"Cows are protection?"

"Strange, isn't it? Cattle are immune. Also goats, sheep, deer, but a cattle pen has traditionally provided the first line of defense at shrines. That's why it's been so dangerous for the liberation to turn temples into their so-called Virtues Gardens. Swarms will escape through portals with nothing to stop them. The wraiths will ride the winds through cities and towns and villages, across fields and forests and plains. Bad times for those caught by their tendrils." He glanced east, where the sun rose over glinting summits. "Humble cattle have spared more than people know. Those who rule now wish folk to forget that the monarchs of old protected them."

"What will happen in Koryu?" she asked.

"Wraiths will have swarmed through the portal there.

The locals will have no defense against them. Except those who, like the August Protector, are immune."

"How are people immune?"

"Anyone with a wraith already nested inside them is safe. Mages, for example."

"Is the August Protector a mage?"

"No. She is immune, just as there are some who do not get ill when a sickness sweeps through a valley or town. I don't know why but I've known others . . ." He paused, eyes flickering and expression shadowed, then swallowed and went on. "I've known others who have the same immunity to wraiths. The difference is, the August Protector chooses to believe it is her virtue that protects her, not chance. That is the problem, do you see?"

Fellian thought of how he had stared at the August Protector with such intensity. "Is she the one you loved, back when you were young?"

"Fellian! Shame on you!" cried Invi. "Apologize!"

Lord Roake gave her a glance that made her feel like a worm. He turned to Shey. "Is Haolu in the infirmary with her ladyship?"

"Yes. I'll go with you." The two men headed off without a glance back.

Invi grabbed Fellian's arm. "Wait with me, rude girl. What were you thinking?"

She watched them walk away side by side with the ease of trusted companions. "Is Shey Lord Roake's son?"

"Has a demon gotten into you and soured your head?"

"No. I just wondered, because that councilwoman told Eirukar that he was a cuckold. Why else would Shey be born to council status and turn his back on it?"

"There's a lot you don't know. I don't fault you for wondering, but by the moon you must learn to not blurt out your poor guesses in front of people. Ask me, in private, if you have questions."

Invi began walking toward the infirmary and, when Fellian did not immediately follow, beckoned. Maybe Invi was annoyed but that didn't mean the water mage would abandon Fellian.

In the early morning sunlight the trees in the orchard took on the benign aspect of welcoming friends. It was good not to be on the run, waiting for a nightmare to drop onto her head. Still, her heart was beating hard and she could tell she would crash soon.

Invi spoke first. "Just to make it clear, Lord Eirukar is Lord Sheykar's sire as well as his father."

"So Shey *is* an eminence after all."

"The Liberationists no longer acknowledge that rank, but yes. His mother is an eminence, a noblewoman from a well-connected court family. A truly beautiful woman in all ways. She sacrificed her life and happiness to marry Eirukar the traitor so we would have an ear and eye on the Liberationist Council. Shey does what he does for love of her."

"Is her name Peony?"

Invi scoffed. "Only peddlers and primitives give their

children cheap plant names like that. Although I suppose young ladies at court might have given each other flowery and poetical nicknames. Since I was never at court I wouldn't know."

"What about you? Where did you come from?"

"A story for another time."

In the asylum Fellian had learned how to tell when people didn't want to talk about themselves. "Well, then, here's a different question. There were eight soldiers who came after us. One fell into a tar pit. Three turned into demons and got killed here. What about the other four? Will they show up here too?"

"The portal is closed."

"Were they left behind in demonland?"

"We call it the realm of aether, but yes, you are correct. Once one portal opens, all open. When it closes, all close. They won't have had time to retrace their path to Koryu's portal."

"What will happen to them?"

"If they are fortunate the wraiths will take them. Then if they survive transformation they may roam in the aether realm as embodied demons, maybe even ones that retain a fragment of their old selves. There is great beauty, as well as terror, in the aether realm. If they don't survive transformation, their flesh and bone will become fodder to birth more swarms."

"But wouldn't any who are immune be able to survive? Can't they open the portal from inside demonland?"

SERVANT MAGE

"Only path breakers can open portals."

"Oh. *Oh*." A chill shivered through her flesh. "So they will be trapped there until the portal is opened again. Is there food and water for people there?"

"You would have to ask the captain how much of the realm of aether has been explored. I think it unlikely. It's a deadly place for those who aren't aetherical beings, even we mages."

"Did they know when they entered? That they were being sent to their deaths?"

"Hard to say. They will have hoped to succeed in their mission. To the August Protector the sacrifice of their lives will have been worth the attempt to kill the child."

Anger built in Fellian like storm clouds piling up against the mountain ridges of her home. "Does that mean people fleeing Koryu might get taken by wraiths? The ones that slipped out through the portal while it was open? That innocent people will turn into demons and go on a rampage that kills more innocent people?"

"It does, Felli."

"So to the captain—his lordship, I mean—all the deaths and havoc these wraiths will cause in the world will be worth it because he saved the child."

Invi gave her a long look, features like still water on a windless day. "Which is why no path breaker opens a portal except in direst need. Of course back in the day, every shrine was protected by a cattle yard and a cohort of blessed moon-children. The August Protector removed

123

those defenses because she claims virtue is the only shield we need. So she'll blame the Monarchists. She'll say if there were no dragon-born, then no portal could ever be opened."

"Is that true?"

Invi sighed.

"So it *is* true? We'd be safe if there were no dragon-born? The Liberationists say the dragon-born call the demons into the land."

"They build a false skin of truth onto a skeleton of lies."

Fellian heard her own voice rising but she couldn't cool down. "You just admitted it's true. That his lordship accepts the deaths of innocents as long as it's in service to his beloved monarchy."

"The aether realm exists whatever the August Protector says. It will not go away even if she murders every five-souled baby. Or if every mage like you and me is indentured or killed. Is that the world you wish for?"

"That's a false question."

Invi chuckled, the wry laughter not mockery but respectful amusement. "What's a true question, then?"

"Why did my grandmother and parents never tell me any of this?"

"Didn't you say they were farmers, not mages?"

"Farmers need to understand soil, weather, seasons, drainage, crops, pests, livestock, and more. Why shouldn't they understand the basics of magecraft too? That there is a realm of aether interwoven with our world?"

"Such secrets are part of the education of a mage. And of priests. It's too complicated and frightening."

"Says who? Shey was surprised I knew how to read because I'm a farmer's daughter. Is reading too complicated too? Or is it just that those in power don't want those they rule to know anything except the lies and half-truths they tell them? It's one thing when people don't want to know. It's another when they aren't allowed to know."

"You've a fierce soul, Felli. I like that about you."

"I like you too, Invi."

"But . . . ? I sense a but."

But they had reached the infirmary.

Ervia had not moved from where Fellian had left her. She stood in sunlight with her face turned toward the heavens and her eyes closed. At the sound of their footfalls, she opened her eyes, smiled shyly at Fellian, and extended a hand as if to greet her with a touch. Just before Fellian could clasp her hand, she pulled back like a skittish horse and looked away, flushed and agitated.

Lord Roake emerged from one of the infirmary doors, without Shey. He carried four mugs as a barmaid would, two in each hand. He paused and looked back as Lady Ilfiantel appeared on the threshold.

"A servus can take ale to your soldiers. Let Gifa call for someone."

"I will do this, as a captain should," he said.

Her frown was swift but resigned. She went back

inside as he headed across the grass toward Fellian and the others.

He offered each a mug as he came up. "Invi. Fellian. Comrade. Drink up."

"How is our Lulu?" Invi asked before Fellian could.

"The bolt is out with minimal disturbance, courtesy of Lady Ilfiantel's great skill as a surgeon. Haolu is unconscious and resting. But the bolt pierced a lung so the prognosis is not good. Yet earth mages have recovered from injuries that would kill anyone else. Only time will tell." He took a long swallow from his own mug. "That's good ale," he remarked, and licked his lips as might any thirsty fellow in a village tavern.

Ervia did not drink but clutched the mug as if it were a priceless treasure. She stared at him as if at light in the darkness. "You are truly Lord Roake? The path breaker? The Wolf's Heart?"

His jaw tightened. His gaze flicked toward the open door, then back to her. "I was called by that name a long time ago."

"Jojen the Wolf," said Fellian as the pieces of the puzzle fell into place. "The one you loved and lost."

Invi nudged her with a foot in warning.

"It's all right," said Lord Roake. "There have never been any such secrets between Lady Ilfiantel and myself. We knew what we each had lost before we agreed to marry."

"You're married to *her*?"

"Felli!"

"Leave it, Invi. There is no reason Fellian could know any of this ancient history, of what happened during the war and in its aftermath. Those of us who lost what we loved best made prudent choices in order to remain loyal to a future that might yet be." Then, miraculously, he looked toward the heavens, as toward hope. He smiled as if his heart had lightened by a bushel weight ten times over. "But now everything has changed. *Everything*."

"Because we rescued the baby?" asked Invi. "One baby is not enough, Captain. We both know it. We are too few. The August Protector's grip is too strong."

"Because I know a secret about the August Protector that she may not yet know herself. Even so brief a time as I touched her skin, I sensed a black rot breeding in her flesh. It will kill her in a few short years, I guarantee it, for I have tracked the progress of a similar disease in other people over the years. When she dies, the council will fall on each other with knives and claws. When they do, we will be ready."

"Ready for what?" asked Fellian.

"For what we have worked for and held on to in secret for all these years," he said in a low and almost hoarse whisper.

His gaze had a shine to it, and it scared her. Not because she was scared of him personally. He was no backstabber, no traitor, no deceiver. He'd die before he would betray his own code of honor. But he had opened a portal to save a child knowing untold others would suffer. The August

Protector's illness—terminal, if he was correct, and there was no reason for Fellian to doubt him—was a portal of another kind. He would open it wide until the maw of a new harsh war engulfed the land again.

The worst of it was, she could not fault him. In his place, she would no doubt do the same. But she was not in his place.

"Invi, I sent Shey up to the manor house to eat and take a nap. Then we must rescue the people trapped in the mines. Fellian is remarkably strong and determined. She can do the work of three Lamps. This is better than I had hoped for."

"What about me?" said Ervia. "Can I become a path breaker? Like you? I hate being an oracle. I hate it when I'm the one who is responsible for children being torn from their families. I'd rather be dead than have to take part in one more census. Please don't make me."

She began to cry silent tears in the manner of a person who knows she'll be whipped if her voice is heard. Such punishments had happened to Fellian too before she had learned silence and hard-heartedness. She wanted to grasp Ervia's hand, to tell her it would be all right somehow, but old habits bit hard. She couldn't bring herself to reveal any vulnerability in the sight of the powerful. And anyway, how could any of them know it would be all right?

"Your life will be different with us," said Lord Roake sternly to Ervia. "We are not the Liberationists. Go with Invi to the mage ward. You'll be cared for . . ." He cocked his head to one side. "But first, tell me. How did you know of the name I was once called?"

Her voice trembled as she spilled her secret. "My aunt. When no one else was around she would sometimes whisper of how things were when she was young. It was forbidden to speak of the old days. Her kinfolk and those they had been married to were all split apart. She and my mother were sent away together. My mother died when I was very young. So Aunt Londria raised me."

He took the mug from her hand, fixed her with a captain's commanding stare. "What is your name?"

Would she refuse to tell him?

But he was not Fellian. Maybe it wasn't Fellian the aether mage had chosen to follow, even though she had allowed herself that rosy dream. Maybe it had been him all along.

"I am named Erlonvia. At the asylum they told me it was an evil name. They called me Ervia instead."

"Erlonvia is a court name. What of your aunt?"

"Aunt Londria?"

"Did she have another name? A house name?"

"I don't know what that is."

"A seal? Jewelry? Any unusual mark?"

The girl bit her lip, decided, and spoke. "She wore a green agate pendant carved with a fort atop a rock. She hid it at census time or when the Rectitude Corps came through the work camp."

He blinked, emptied his mug on a single swig, then

said, "By the Moon, child. Are you speaking of my second cousin Ulondria? She was fourth in line for the headship of House Roake. I am now lord of House Roake but I was only of a minor branch before the war. Those who weren't killed outright went into hiding or took false names to disguise who they were. I searched but never found the missing. Where did you grow up?"

"In the Agtipti marshlands. All flies and pestilence. The nearest town was a three-day walk but we were not allowed to travel there. I never saw another place until they took me to the asylum in Alabaster City."

His smile was startling in its brightness, as appealing as the sun after days of rain. "This is another Moon-blessed gift to our cause. We are kin, you and I, Erlonvia. Does your aunt live?"

"She did, when I was taken. That was five years ago."

"We will get her back, I promise you. I'll take you myself to the manor house. You will receive all the care a young woman of your rank deserves."

She stared at him, too stunned by this turn of fortune to answer.

Lord Roake gave Invi what Fellian had mistaken all this time for a captain's nod, and it was a commander's decisiveness but now she understood that wasn't all it was. It was the command of a noble to one who can never be a noble, however trusted or gifted they might be. "Take Fellian to the mage ward. Feed her, see she has a space to nap. We depart as soon as I can assemble wagons and an escort."

"Yes, Captain," said Invi. "Come along, Felli."

Fellian had watched them leave, first Haolu, then Shey, now Ervia. Erlonvia. She slipped out the knife she'd stolen and offered it, hilt first. "You might need this. Think of it as a gift."

Erlonvia met Fellian's eyes in the remembered way, separated by a wall. Only now, looking intently and from this close, did Fellian see the thread of aetherical silver ringing her iris. Erlonvia glanced at the captain for permission. When he gave a nod, she closed her fingers awkwardly over the knife's hilt.

Invi frowned, looking between the two of them. "Was there something more you wanted to say, Fellian?"

"There's nothing more I have to say."

10

And it was true. Her words deserted her, fled like shadows at midday. The glare of this new sunlight was too hot, too bright.

A priest escorted them to the gate. The guard on duty eyed her and Invi. He said, "Are you the water mage who saved Lord Roake and the last cohort at Kadastra Ford?"

"I might be," said Invi with a congenial smile.

"They say you were stuck in a Liberationist prison for ten years. Lord Roake never stopped trying to find you and get you out. And here you are."

"Here I am, and grateful for it."

"Did he find a Lamp?" He glanced at Fellian.

Fellian said nothing. From the outer portico, a road led into a valley enclosed by jagged cliffs on all sides. To the west, mountains formed in an icy wall. The view to the north shocked her with its familiarity. Past the two-peaked mountain her people called Old Goat, and beyond the jagged notch called Eagle's Nest in the high saddle ridge, lay a borderlands province called Exiles' Tears. *Home.* Her chest tightened although she did not cry. She'd long since given up tears. At this time of year she could cross without dying in the snow that would start falling in earnest in another month.

Invi said, "Yes, she is a Lamp."

"Wonderful news! We lost all our Lamps at the siege

of Ogira," the man confided with a friendly nod at Fellian that almost melted the weight on her tongue. "That's how our people came to be trapped in the mines. All we need is a single strong Lamp to light their way across the Gullet."

Curiosity unsheathed its persistent claws. What was a gullet? And what about Invi? Ten years in a Liberationist prison!

Invi said to the priest, "I can make my own way from here," and went down the steps.

Fellian followed. The valley was striped with fields lush with ripe crops under the morning sun. Clusters of sod houses stood along the length of the vale, oddly quiet, as if they were empty shells waiting to be filled. In the distance a sprawling smithy and its furnace puffed smoke. On the slopes, sheep tended grassy pastures. Nearer at hand rose a palatial compound that must have been the manor house, with two full stories and a stable with a covered outdoor exercise yard where horses were being ridden.

Invi whistled a cheerful tune as they approached a village with its central square, a covered market and weaving hall, and a barracks. West of the village amid a field of poppies stood a modest single-story compound wrapped around a large courtyard. A woman wearing a dark green surcoat waited at the entrance, face pinched in a severe expression. She held a fly whisk, braided with what Fellian was certain was human hair, and flicked it as they arrived.

"How can I know you are Invi the Face Stealer? No one really knows what a face stealer looks like, do they?"

"Maybe they don't, but they know for sure where the persimmons are hidden."

The fly whisk woman's frown split into a wide grin. She embraced the Water Adept. The two laughed and gabbled as Fellian waited. Her head ached. The sting of a blister burned on her right heel. Her fingers were cold because she had taken off her gloves at Koryu to form Lamps and forgotten to put them back on, or maybe she had lost them in the aether realm.

The woman pulled away, wiping her eyes. "I thought Lord Roake's expedition ill-conceived but since it has brought you back after all you must have endured, my dear friend, I cannot be angry." She indicated Fellian with her fly whisk. "I suppose it is too much to hope you are a Lamp so we might rescue those poor refugees before they die in darkness."

Was Haolu dead? If she did die, would her sacrifice be celebrated as another brave soul whose lost light illuminated the noble story?

"Wraith got her tongue?"

Invi cocked a measuring look. "She's usually overspilling with sharp questions and impertinent retorts but she needs food and what sleep she can grab before they go in."

"You're not going?"

"I've had enough walls."

"I suppose you have. They don't need you for this."

"Come on, Felli. Let's get the grime of our travels washed

off while Mormi here—she's an Earth Adept—sends a servus to the kitchen to get you a tray of food."

The compound was what they called a mage ward, with the usual institutional common rooms: a latrine out back, a baths chamber, sleeping halls, classrooms. After they washed, Invi showed her where to store her pack, which she carefully wrapped in a spiky rope of Lamplight.

"You don't need that here," said Invi with a wry smile, "but I understand why you feel more comfortable protecting your gear. Let's get some food into you."

The interior courtyard was cut into four unevenly sized quarters by two crossing colonnades. With a gaggle of on-lookers keeping their distance as they stared at her, Fellian sat on a bench at a table. Invi left her there, chased away the onlookers, and went back inside. A boy in a wool tunic brought a tray of food.

"My thanks," Fellian said, scraping the rust out of her voice. "I'm called Fellian. What may I call you?"

He ducked his chin. "My apologies if I have offended you, mageborn. I answer to servus, as I would not wish to bother you with my humble name. I shall fetch a mug of sweet tea for you now." He hurried off.

Fellian stared at the bowl of scallion-and-barley gruel, two thick slices of rye bread, and a dill-flavored wedge of sheep's cheese. Her gut sat heavy from the terrifying rush of events compounded by annoyance at a boy who refused to offer her the most basic decency as she had learned at her grandmother's knee: the exchange of names as an act of people whose worth before the gods had equal weight. Maybe he was afraid to. Maybe it wasn't allowed by the customs of this place.

She ate and drank with an effort, knowing she must keep up her strength. Afterward an elderly servus led her to a pallet in one of the sleeping halls, where she curled up and closed her eyes, then was shaken awake by Invi before she realized she'd fallen asleep.

"Felli, it's time to go. Here's a set of clothing for you. It's ordinary farmer's garb for now but we'll get you set up with a mage tunic and tabard. You needn't wear Liberationist garb ever again. What do you think of that?"

Fellian shrugged. The clothing was warm and well made, eminently suitable.

Invi sighed but did not address her as they left the mage ward. A party of soldiers and wagons waited in the village square. Lord Roake had cleaned up and changed into a bold military jacket of black trimmed with silver. He sat on a bay mare with the ease of a man who has never had to fear being beaten for daring to ride. He gave Fellian a nod but did not otherwise greet her as he gave directions to the headman of the village, who was preparing to receive the refugees. If they could save them.

With his lordship at the front, the procession headed down a rugged track that led into a southward spur of the valley. Fields gave way to scrubland pockmarked by stumps of trees grown round with sweet-wire, brambles, scorch grass, and bitter-fall, a tempting pasturage for the goats who watched their procession with interest.

A horse came galloping. On it, dashing in a black-and-silver jacket, rode Shey. Lord Sheykar. He passed the main group to fall in beside Lord Roake. After they exchanged words, Shey searched the column until he spotted her. Dismounting, he fell in to walk beside her.

"I hope you ate and rested well, Fellian."

She walked.

"Have I done something to offend you?"

"What news of Haolu?"

"No news. What a business about Erlonvia though! I mean, everyone knew Roake was the one who saved the life of Jojen the Wolf. That was before anyone had any idea it was she who would turn the tide and defeat the Liberationist army at the Stammering Gates. But because of that and because my cursed father was in love with her too, with the Wolf, I mean. Not that a turd like my father would ever have a chance with a blessed hero like her. Anyway, all the eminent houses were persecuted after the August Protector's victory but Roake House especially. So to find one of the lost heirs to House Roake, to get word of her aunt and that she's alive. It's a blessing. They're already talking about—"

He broke off. They'd fallen behind the others and it was obvious to Fellian the soldiers and wagoners saw it happening and let it be. Shey looked at her expectantly. Her thoughts were a stew churned by a ceaseless spoon but she said nothing. Her silence was all the invitation he needed.

KATE ELLIOTT

"With her lineage, and mine, of course they're match-making already. It would be a prudent arrangement. Good for the cause. But she's not my type," he finished with a sidelong glance at her with his pretty eyes and an inviting lift of his handsome mouth.

"I'm not your type either."

He held his tongue with the silence of a man who knows he's put a foot wrong but can't figure out how to get free without losing his boot to the muck. The spur of valley narrowed to become a defile between two rocky ridges grown thick with trees. Fresh logging scars ate into the forest. Ahead, the soldiers started singing an old song she hadn't heard since she was a child: *"Beneath the wings of the night, moonlight pours through the open window. Blessed goddess, fill our hearts with your strength."*

His tone softened, turned coaxing, as he tried again. "There's an old tradition among eminences about people who marry according to the needs of the lineage but take a heart spouse. Like Lord Roake did . . . well, he wasn't married at the time he met the Wolf but he had been betrothed a few years earlier. The rebellion threw all of their lives over in a heap . . ."

"And his heart spouse, the blessed—or cursed—hero Jojen the Wolf, died in the end, didn't she?"

His silence lasted longer as he wrestled through untidy thoughts. She offered no encouragement. She just walked.

"Lord Roake says you're an unusually powerful Lamp because you're strong-minded and unafraid to experiment.

He respects you." He left space for her to reply. When she didn't, he went on. "The new queen will need a five-arrow quiver. That's the tradition, to assign five mages to guard and raise each royal child. You could ask for that privilege even though you're not from an eminent house, because he favors you and you helped rescue her. That counts for a great deal. If I made the same request . . . I mean after I get my mother out of the capital, away from my father and that poisonous council, now that her cover is broken . . . then you and I would be comrades as we've been on this journey. We would be working together."

She trudged after the wagons as they rattled along a rocky path amid the tang of pine and spruce. Ahead rose a stark cliff face, a dead end.

"I'm speaking too soon. It's early days, I know that. We really are barely acquainted but I've just been so amazed by how your unquenchable spirit survived after everything you've been through. Your bold speaking. I've never seen anyone who looks like you. Gifa says you're a honey bloom, a hill sprite. Cousin to demons but woven of magic and tree sap and scented fog, right out of the tales."

She'd heard the term enough that it no longer made her flinch. On her mother's side, yes. Her people had always lived in the hill country. Her fathers' ancestors down one line were the newcomers, dissidents sent north over the pass into territory occupied by Monarchist armies a mere four generations ago. Most had wept to be exiled to a place so foreign to their understanding. One great-grandfather had pragmatically got on with the work of living by marrying into a local household as a second father. He hadn't cared about the scandal it caused among his own kin, for whom the idea of a woman having two husbands was shocking and embarrassing. He'd never looked back, and she couldn't trace her line of descent past him on that branch because he'd made such a clean break of it. Or maybe his people had made a clean break of him while clinging to their memories of the land they prayed to return to someday.

"You're so quiet today. I know it's a lot to take in." Shey smiled with something like bashfulness, an appealing look on a man with a face like his. Handsome men in particular annoyed her because at first she'd believed their entreaties. She'd learned that the hard way, when she was at her most vulnerable.

He added, "I have a duty to my mother and to the cause. I'll fulfill that. But it doesn't mean people can't find ways to be happy where there's a promise of joy. But we have hope now. We have hope to light a Lamp for a better future, isn't that right?"

"I'm here to finish the job I promised to the captain in exchange for a travel license, money, and supplies."

He raised both hands as if fending off an attack, although her tone had been softer than his.

She added, "Please explain what I can expect to find ahead and what I'll need to do."

He glanced sidelong at her again with the look of a man who hasn't given up. "All you have to do is light the way."

The path ended at a cleft in the rock face. Here they left the wagons, oxen, and drivers. The cleft let into a cavern through which strange shrill winds whistled. The air held a charge that pricked like pins on her skin. They'd brought no oil or lanterns so she made a Lamp. Lord Roake walked beside her as they set off into a tunnel. It led deep into the rock, down a long, smooth ramp with those mournful winds singing into their faces. Rings driven into the rock face allowed a rope railing to be strung down the ramp into the darkness.

At one-hundred-pace intervals a shallow alcove had been dug into the tunnel wall and an iron stand set on heavy iron feet. At each she wove a new Lamp and knotted it to the iron so it would not drift off. Her time working at the establishment had taught her to gauge how best to light a chamber for the several night bells a luxurious supper between gossiping comrades would last. That way she need not reenter to replenish its light. The drunker they got the better it was to avoid them.

The sting of the winds grew worse the deeper they descended. She wept because the air whipped tears from her eyes.

"Everyone is ready," said a soldier who had been waiting in the darkness at the end of the tunnel.

The passage opened onto a wide ledge. Lord Roake set a hand on her arm to halt her as her Lamp was buffeted by a powerful updraft that tore it out of her reach and bore it up and up, swirling until it caught against an unseen barrier.

The soldiers spread out behind them, backs to the ledge's cliff wall. The space before and above her was vast. At her feet a chasm split the rock. From its depths thundered the steady roar of a mighty cataract that sprayed not water but a noxious invisible presence. Not the aether swarms but something she'd never before experienced. So many mysteries in the world.

Lord Roake said, "No flame will burn here but a Lamp will. There are five iron arches fixed to the ledge. If you wreath each in Lamplight—"

"A clear line of sight and a landmark within the Eye," she interrupted. "I understand now. There's no way across the chasm without a Lamplighter, and you lost all your Lamps. That's why your people are stuck over there."

A voice hailed them out of the darkness, heard faintly across the boom and clamor. "Is it true, what the herald told us? Are we finally safe? We've had our first deaths. We're out of food."

"We are here, and we have a Lamp," called Lord Roake. "Send waves of strong with weak to help them to the surface. Fellian, if you will."

All that long journey, and in the end she had to do nothing more than what she had done every night at the establishment in Qen for the entertainment of its monied and therefore virtuous patrons. She wove light into the five arches, made of them bright gateways visible across the crevasse.

So they came: weary refugees, wounded soldiers, silent

children, and stubborn elders. It was a slow process because one Eye could hold open for no more than eight or ten to pass through.

Shey shifted from foot to foot beside Lord Roake, at last bursting out, "Can we not thread the needle and get me across so I can help? I can hold Eyes open longer than any of these air mages. We could get more through faster."

"There's no gain in using you compared to the risk of threading the needle. Not when we know they're safe now, even though it takes time. Let that be a lesson for what lies ahead. Patience." He glanced at Fellian, who was listening as she twisted a new Lamp into life between her hands to refresh one of the blazing archways. "Shey, go up to the wagons. Get the wounded and the weakest to the infirmary at once. We'll follow once everyone is across."

Shey gave Fellian a searching look, an unasked question.

"Go!"

Shey went, making his way upward through the slow-moving refugees.

"I hope he is not proving a nuisance to you, Fellian. I can speak to him, if necessary."

"I'm fine."

He had the knack of not pressing. Anyway, he had other work at hand. Folk who knelt before him to give thanks and fealty. A captain at arms who gave a grim report about fifty refugees and their squad of guards who'd been cut off from the main group and fallen into the hands of the Liberationists. A priest who was an old boon comrade; they touched foreheads in a gesture of loyalty outlawed by the council. A clerk with a tally board rigged for darkness, on which she held a census of every soul who had been waiting on the other side, including three deaths and a missing child whom everyone feared had fallen into the crevasse: 1,247 people, of whom half were of an age to fight.

"How did they stop the Liberationists from following them here?" Fellian asked, for the question gnawed straight through her determination to stop talking.

"As you will have guessed, these ancient mines have offered an access to our hidden refuge for a long time. This group was forced to block the main tunnel with a rockfall so as not to be overrun. The rebels are chipping away at rocks and will eventually get through, though they'll take casualties in the doing. But they can never cross the chasm."

"Not without an ally on this side."

He tipped a measuring gaze at her. "That ally would have to be a Lamp. You can be sure I chose you carefully from the list I was given."

"You are a careful planner, Captain. But the stories people tell of you make you out to be so different. A reckless, fearless risk-taker barely a step ahead of death."

"In the early days I dared much because I did not care if I lived or died. That has all changed. Everything has changed."

"The August Protector said one by itself isn't enough, that you need two."

His gaze drifted up to her lost Lamp, like a drifting firefly, caught so far above them it might as well have risen into another world because it was out of her reach.

"You have another one hidden somewhere," she whispered.

"All these years I have dreamed of this day," he murmured to himself, as if he'd forgotten she was there. Abruptly she hoped he had not heard her muttered words, nor did she repeat them.

"Lord Roake!" The clerk hurried up, tally board raised triumphantly. She knelt before him as tears coursed down her wrinkled cheeks. "They're all across, your lordship. All accounted for."

His gaze hung a moment longer on the distant light, then snapped back to earth. "Close them down, Fellian. We're done here."

He spoke clear and firm, with no accusing query in his eyes. He hadn't heard her.

They ascended Lamp by Lamp as she took the light back into her, leaving impenetrable darkness behind. He took the rear guard, walking three paces behind her, nothing between him and the tumultuous abyss. She understood now what he'd always had, starting on the day thirty years ago when he had chosen not to lay down his sword. He'd always had something to protect. Something no one else knew about.

With most of the day now past, shadows drenched the defile. The sun had long since fallen below the ridgeline. The air bore a mountainous chill. Lanterns swayed from wagons headed back up the defile, burning with the ordinary light of flame. A squad of waiting soldiers held his lordship's horse, but he did not mount, instead walking at a strong pace that allowed him to advance past the slow-moving wagons like a shepherd counting his herd. So many wished to speak to Lord Roake on the path up the defile and out the spur and back to the village, the temple, and the manor house. Their reports. Who had died. Documents rescued. A bag of precious gems that could be dispersed to buy armor, weapons, and maybe even horses. A noted drill sergeant who'd been living disguised as a baker, ready to begin training over five hundred young people eager to enroll as new recruits. Ten young earth roughs had been identified as well as two earth servant mages who had defected from the Liberationist army, an elderly air mage who had been living in hiding, and two fire roughs eager for training.

"Do you think I can ride the horse since his lordship is walking?" Fellian asked one of the soldiers.

"Of course not. This is his lordship's horse."

"I'm really tired."

"There's room in one of the wagons, mage. Our thanks to you."

Not thanks enough. She walked. A pair of soldiers stuck with her as she trudged along. Mercifully they did not attempt to converse with her. Even tired as she was she slowly outpaced the wagons at the rear laden with wounded, ill, and exhausted. Even the sickest looked alight with jubilation and determination. For their sakes she was glad of it, each one a soul pried from the grip of the liberation. That was victory enough for today. As they came into view of the valley and its twinkling lanterns they broke into song, a hymn to moon and dragon she'd never before heard, oddly moving and yet in her heart so remote.

She walked on, with her escort trailing her. First she went to the mage ward where she grabbed her pack and after that to the infirmary. The area was bustling as wounded soldiers were brought in. Lanterns blazed everywhere.

"Where's Haolu?" she asked an orderly.

"Who? We're busy here, can't you see?"

"The earth mage who was shot in the lung."

The answer was a flick of a hand toward the far end of the infirmary block. She walked to the last room, the soldiers trailing her at a polite distance. A propped-open door led into a chamber with four cots. The room was musty, as if it was usually closed up, but the floor was clean.

An elderly servus sat in a chair beside a burning candle, knitting. Fellian was learning how to recognize people's status according to the way they were dressed. She looked up as Fellian took a cautious step inside. "Who are you?"

Fellian spotted the patient on a cot in a corner. Haolu wore only a linen shift for she burned with fever, but even so the heat was fading in her limbs, her hands and feet going cold as her body pulled its last resources into her core.

"She came with his lordship," said the servus. "She'll die a hero for helping to rescue the young monarch. A Water

Adept sat with her all the afternoon. I'm to sit here over the night or until she passes. His lordship says no one should die alone."

"We all die alone." Fellian thought of Mother and Older Father, how she'd watched them fight at first for each choked breath until finally their gazes had withdrawn from the world down the tunnel of death as all do in the end, leaving the living behind. "I'll sit with her, if you have other tasks."

"Are you sure?"

"I'd like to. Is anyone coming to check on her?"

"Lady Ilfiantel says there's nothing more can be done except make her comfortable. And she'd know. She's saved many thought past saving, and lost fewer than most. She's the best battle surgeon in the land."

"Is that why Lord Roake married her? To patch up his soldiers?"

"Beneficial to all involved, as she was a widow with three children," the woman agreed amiably. "There is a lot of work to do with all these new arrivals. If you don't mind . . ."

"Go ahead."

After the woman gathered up her knitting and left, Fellian found her tight chest eased. She knelt beside the cot and touched Haolu's slack face. The slurred breathing came in ragged bursts followed by long pauses. She wrapped the earth mage's hand with her own, feeling skin that like hers bore the calluses of a person who has worked from an early age.

"I'm here, Lulu. Did you mind being called that? It didn't seem you did. Invi has the knack of making a person feel comfortable. You were right about what you said. *March with shoulders back. Look people right in the eye.*"

She was babbling but despite what she had said to the servus she couldn't bear for Haolu to die in silence, untouched, ignored. So she sat on her heels on the stone floor and talked until she fell asleep, slumped against the side of the cot.

In the middle of the night a murmur of voices woke her.

"My lord, you must rest. There's already someone in attendance."

Fellian pried open her eyes to see a candle's soft aura and, within it, the stern features of the captain illuminated half in shadow and half in pale light as he entered. He nodded to acknowledge her before he draped a wreath of leaves and flowers across Haolu's barely rising and falling chest beneath her chin: an old custom said to sweeten dying.

As he left she heard him say to his attendants, "Always show honor to those who give their lives. Don't leave it to another's hand if you are the one who commanded them."

The wreath had an overpowering and soporific scent that chased her down into restless dreams. When she woke, Haolu was dead, breath-less, her heat fading.

Stiffly Fellian rose. Outside the light was gray with

dawn. The same two soldiers stood by the door, looking tired but with the rising light in their faces.

"Apprentice," said the elder soldier in polite greeting.

So she was now an apprentice mage. The servant mage had vanished like smoke blown away on a fresh wind.

"We've been asked to make sure you are fed. After that, his lordship wishes you to be brought to the audience hall."

They escorted her to the manor house, not through the front gate but around to a kitchen wing. In a simply furnished eating hall enlivened by excited chatter she ate oat porridge, rye bread hot from the oven, and cheese. No one sat with her; people were either working or seated at other tables according to a complex system she did not understand, although it seemed those of servus rank did not feel free to sit at the same table as a mage. The soldiers also refused her invitation to sit. "We eat at the barracks."

Still lugging her pack she followed them down a passageway into the residential wing of the manor house, abuzz with activity for it seemed every eminence in the valley had to live in this compound since there were no other stately houses. She and the soldiers entered the audience hall through a modest side door.

Like the eating hall, the audience hall had a lofty beamed ceiling, with windows set high along the wall. Everything else about the two halls differed. Tapestries hung on the walls below the windows, depicting the same battle she had seen every day in the privy courtyard. The central pair of tapestries hung behind the dais with its chairs. In this rendition of the battle, no noble ditchdigger struck a blow for liberation. Instead a nobly garbed man stabbed the dragon monarch in the back. The young barbarian known as Jojen the Wolf was being swarmed by a squad of shouting Liberationists as she cut about her with an ax. At her side a youth no older than she was shielded her from their blows.

Lord Roake sat in a chair with his back to the battle scene. Built of sturdy, dark-grained wood, the chair was not a throne but a seat meant to last through the storm of years. Beside him a white-haired elder in a silver-white ribbon-trimmed surcoat sat next to a cradle, rocking it with a foot. Fellian did not at first recognize the young woman seated next to his lordship, wearing a gracious linen gown ornamented by a silver sash and with her dark hair neatly braided and pinned back beneath a silver circlet. But her brow and the scar revealed her. When she caught sight of Fellian, she brushed a hand over a knife hilt sheathed in a gold-trimmed scabbard. But there was no way of knowing why, or what she was thinking. As Grandmother often said, *What you believe you know of another's thoughts is generally just your own hanging in front of you.*

The main doors opened to admit a procession of people in surcoats like those of the elder at the cradle. At the front strode Shey, wearing a gold surcoat and a silver circlet, followed by three other mages wearing circlets. Behind walked a smiling Invi, in a blue surcoat trimmed with ribbons at the shoulders, and beside the water mage the woman in green who'd met Fellian and Invi at the mage ward's gate. A gaggle of blues and greens followed. Most lacked ribbons, so Fellian guessed they were apprentice mages unmarked by extra ornamentation. At the tail end squirmed a nervous and excited pack of brown-surcoated roughs.

Lord Roake rose to receive them. He gestured toward Fellian. Of course he had seen her, although he'd given no sign.

"I recognize the ward of mages, who shield the monarch we serve. Fellian, they have come to welcome you into the ward. You are a powerful Lamp, with great potential, a keen mind, and a fierce tenacity that will serve you well in the years to come. You can at last be trained as you deserve. You can rise as far as your determination and effort will take you. In the name of the monarch, and for my own part, as commander of her forces and guardian of the honor of our land, I ask you to join us."

Us.

For five years she had survived by wrapping herself as in armor made by magic to keep the worst away. She, who had grown up in the border hills where her extended kin could be found in every village along the high paths, had kept her name to herself and offered her trust to only a handful. Even then, that trust had been betrayed twice. It was so hard to stand alone. The mages stood as if they were a gathering of clans, bound by a greater purpose and a kinship rooted in the bones, not in blood.

Shey's chin came up as a grin played on his lips. Invi caught her gaze and smiled. Shy Erlonvia cast a skittish gaze at her, and blushed.

As if lifted on the wings of celebratory music, a vision of a future unfolded. Praised and feted, comrades in arms. What awaited her in the hills she could not know: two parents executed in disgrace, Grandmother in prison or dead, Younger Father's fate unknown.

But the exiles who wept in the province known as Exiles' Tears were the ones who had come from the outside. They were not the ones bound to the land and its network of kinship. Whatever awaited her in the hills, it included people who knew her name and what it meant.

"This is not my road," she said.

"Fellian!" cried Shey. "What about—"

At a glance from Lord Roake he clamped down his lips and glared at her with entreaty in his eyes.

"Captain, I am grateful for the rescue but you have misunderstood me and who I am. My parents were arrested and executed for sedition. Not for speaking against the Liberationists, even though it's true they considered the council unjust and cruel. But they didn't wish for a restored monarchy. They were executed because they taught people to read without having a license from the council. They applied for one but were denied because they weren't deemed virtuous enough. Under the monarchy, my grandmother and her sisters applied for a license to teach. In those days a license was only available to people who had taken the

chancery examinations. The exams were only open to people born into eminent households. Virtue or rank, what's
the difference to those never allowed to have either? So my
people—my simple farming and shepherding hill people—
taught in secret any who wished to learn. My parents were
executed for rebelling against authority. I was meant to be
sent to a labor camp with my grandmother, but an oracle
discovered I was a fire rough. That's my story."

Invi sighed.

Again Lord Roake caught Shey's eye and shook his
head. Shey cast her a heartrending look but he obeyed and
said no more. Erlonvia looked stricken, and bent her head
to stare at her folded, compliant hands.

"I did what I promised, Captain. Now I want what you
promised me."

11

A hidden overland route led out of the valley through a tunnel, a fort, and across a drawbridge that spanned a river raging through a defile. On the other side of the bridge, soldiers dressed as shepherds blindfolded her and sat her in a cart. After most of a day of jolting travel, they released her on the road that led over Exiles' Pass.

She headed north into late-afternoon shadows beneath a cloud-streaked sky. Her pack bumped merrily but annoyingly on her back until she tightened its straps. This late in the day she passed no one headed south, by which she deduced that the next crossing inn lay close ahead. So it proved when she reached a distance marker, a bronze plaque affixed to a pillar. To her surprise the market town of Zaren lay a day's travel south, which meant the hidden valley was farther north than she'd realized. She was already halfway home.

It made her wonder where the valley was located, and if she could find it again. It made her wonder what Lord Roake's plans were. Would he build his army and, when the August Protector was too sick to command, strike south to Alabaster City to decapitate the council before they could agree on a successor? Or would he take over the outlying territories like a tightening noose until he could strangle the Liberationist hold? And then what would happen? He would succeed or he would fail. Maybe he and the young monarch he now acted as regent for would restore integrity to the court.

None of that changed things for her. What made a person a mage? It was the work that made you a mage. She could have lived her entire life as a fire rough with a knack for sensing people and animals at night, even if she wouldn't have understood why. A mage like her had only one soul-wraith nested inside her, as opposed to five. Even so, the most significant difference between the infant and her was that people were determined to offer the child the best possible education and training, treating the baby with not just respect but awe.

What made a newborn baby a monarch? Only that people said it was. Meanwhile, the life of Nish's uncle Oran would have been even worse if the Liberationists had discovered the mage gift he worked so hard to hide.

She caught up to a group of travelers as they came to a post town and its barrier gate. Stone houses lined either side of the road with garden strips terraced into the steep hillsides behind. The travelers were peddlers, merchants, and clerks about official business, having clumped together on the journey for a sense of security. She squeezed in among them with a quiet smile. At the guard station she handed over travel papers that identified her as a servant courier carrying a nonurgent directive from the Liberationist Council in Alabaster City for the council of Ellibozia, the farthest northern town in the land. After the Monarchists had conquered the hill country they'd built

Ellibozia right at the edge of the impenetrable monster-ridden and fume-drenched forest known as the Wilderness of Sin, a place her people had long avoided.

She walked down the post town's street until she found a humble lodging house decorated with a spray of the prickly but beautiful flowers commonly known as thistle-bright but which her people called by its old name, fellian. The plant was a symbol of the old kinship lines because it grew on the rockiest, harshest ground and was hard to kill.

A woman came out onto the porch with a broom, eyeing her.

"Peace in the evening, aunt," said Fellian in the old way taught to her by her grandmother, in which all people within the lineages were woven together in a greater kinship of shared language and traditions. The words felt rusty on her tongue. What if she had got them wrong or mistaken the meaning of the proprietor hanging a sprig of fellian?

The woman nodded. "May you find peace, niece. Do you need lodging? A secure bunk for the night?"

"My thanks. I do."

So it went for four days as she walked, able each night to find a lodging house where she felt safe. Late summer and early autumn was the prime traveling season because of the lack of snow on the high pass, so she never walked alone on the road.

On the fifth day she reached a small market town, a trading center where people came out of the hills to trade furs, wool, live raptors and claw-wells, dried freshwater fish, polished beads, and a rare aromatic wood. As soon as she'd been old enough to make the trek she'd accompanied Younger Father twice each summer on the long hill path from their home valley to this very market to trade the narcotic dream-berries loved by southerners. She'd already planned out her route. In the morning she'd leave the main road and head into the hills, away from the regulation of the government. Up on the tangled paths she could overnight with kin who lived in hamlets tucked into the crevices and terraces of the hills.

Home. Home. She was home.

With cheeks flushed and heart racing, she sparked the interest of the guards for the first time.

"You're from these parts," they said, examining her face. "What makes you so nervous, honey girl?"

"Out of breath from the climb." She wiped her brow. "I've been running messages down on the plain. My legs hurt."

They laughed, and their sergeant invited her to a soak in the hot baths with him after he got off duty. At that very instant, as she was struggling to figure out what to say to not anger a man who had the power to arrest her on a whim, she saw her father.

Younger Father, of course: the authorities had never fathomed the custom of one woman marrying two men, usually brothers or cousins. So when they'd arrested Mother and traced her sedition to her household, they'd brought in her mother, her daughter, and her husband, and never even recognized she had a second husband.

There he stood on the porch of a trading house, head cocked in the way he had when he was listening, to cant his good ear toward the sound.

She raised her gaze to the gloating sergeant. She leaned a bit closer and said, in a low voice, "Councilman Eirukar might be offended if you disturb what he keeps for his own amusement, Sergeant. I recommend you look elsewhere."

"Why would a high council member's plaything be couriering messages to distant provinces instead of sitting in silk in a love nest?"

"Do you want to ask him?" She met his gaze. Maybe it was her honest anger, or maybe it was the hot curling thread of the wraith born nested into soft baby bones now gone hard. Maybe he was a prudent man who feared the arbitrary power of the council.

He laughed in a mocking voice and waved her forward. She did not look over her shoulder but the shadow of his contempt and lust stalked at her back.

Her father had gone inside the trading house. It was agony to walk at an ordinary pace so as not to betray haste. It took a thousand years to get there, but at last she set foot on the porch.

A woman stepped out with a broom in hand and said, politely, "Niece, we aren't a lodging house. They are farther down the road by the northern gate." Then she hesitated, looked more closely, and added, "Do I know you?"

Voice choking in her throat, terrified she'd lost him forever, fallen into the boiling tar pit, Fellian pushed rudely past into the interior. Windows deep-set into thick walls allowed daylight to streak the cold flagstone floor and the shelves and display baskets. A clerk's table for the proprietor with its scales, measuring rod, and knife sat at the back in front of a curtain. Panic flooded her until it burned in her chest and her hands grew warm. He wasn't there. She'd mistaken him, seen his face on the body of another as if a water mage had stolen her dreams, her hopes, her last rope and handhold.

All the swollen years of cruelty endured by clinging to that tiny sticky patch of hope burst and spilled its venom into her heart. She sobbed as her courage gave way.

A hand caught her under the elbow. "Now then, child, I do think I know you. Aren't you called Fellian? Of the indigo tiger lineage through your mother?"

In the drifting shadow and light of the high-raftered chamber and its dense smells of mountain herbs and old wool, through the blurring tears, Fellian saw the woman's face as a landmark. The trading house was familiar from the long-ago expeditions she'd taken with Younger Father: the smell of bitter-fall and ease-wort hit her hard, a cascade of memories dropping onto her head. Years ago she'd caught a glimpse of him on the porch; maybe the yearning had pushed the image into her mind's eye as if hope could make it real.

He wasn't here. But she knew this woman.

"Diyana," Fellian said, testing the name. "Of the cerulean wolf lineage through your mother."

"You were taken away to an asylum after the executions at Indigo Rock," said Diyana, peering at her with the greatest intensity. "Five years back, wasn't it? You were just a child."

"I can't go back. I won't go back." She twisted, thinking to pull her elbow away and run, but Diyana released her and spoke kindly.

"You are a fugitive, then?" She glanced at the door open to the porch and the street beyond. "Let's get you into the back."

"I thought I saw my father. We used to come here to trade at Long Sun and at Harvest's End."

"You've got to get out of the public room." Diyana tugged her past the curtain into a dim passage lined with six doors. Once there she said in a low voice, "Miyar is not here."

"But he was here?"

"Last month at the Long Sun, yes."

"He's alive." Her voice cracked on the words.

"Yes. The authorities never took him. Of course we never told."

Pain burst in her chest like the cracking of her sternum punched from the inside with sheer, utter, unstoppable, unbearable emotion. She had to lean against the wall as waves of despair and grief and agonizing joy crashed through her until she thought she would faint from the weight of believing there was something left for her. Not just roots in stony ground too stubborn to give up. A chance to flourish.

Diyana waited.

At length the dizziness and weight eased and Fellian could speak again. "My grandmother? Do you know anything of her?"

"Yes. After three years in prison in Ellibozia she became very ill and was released. The hill air revived her. She lives still."

She had to fight to breathe through ragged pants, and slowly measured her air so again she could talk. "How do you know?"

"I know because Miyar married my sister two years ago. Leha, if you recall her. Your mother's mother lives with them. I see Miyar every month these days. He always speaks about you, niece. If there are any servant mages passing through he asks if they know of you. Just a year ago he spoke to an earth mage who said he had been at the asylum with you. That gave him hope you are still alive." She warmed to her tale, chafing Fellian's cold hands between her own. "He's been saving to buy a trade license so he can take dream-berries direct to Alabaster City on his own. He'd tell the authorities it is to make a better profit by not being forced to trade with a middleman. But really it would be to seek news of you and other children who were taken. He can pass as a southern man."

The words made Fellian giddy. Of course it was what he would do. "How many have been taken? There were two with me, five years ago. They were sent to a different asylum."

"There's a list, held in secret. That's all I know. Are you finished with your mage service?"

"No. I escaped."

"The chancery will send the Rectitude killers after you."

"I know."

"Any persons accused of helping an escaped servant mage will be punished."

"I won't go back. I can buy supplies and leave, no one the wiser, no reason to trace me here. I understand you have to protect this trading house. But . . ." She trailed off.

"But?"

"I do not wish to cause any trouble for *you*, aunt."

The heat in Diyana's face shifted minutely. "Who is it you intend to cause trouble for?"

"People can hide in the hills. They've done it before."

"That's not what I mean. You are a lot like your grandmother, you know. Once an idea takes root, it does not let go."

There could be no half measures. "Things are going to change."

"How so?"

She was home. This woman was kin.

"The August Protector is dying. The Liberationist Council will battle one another for power because they are greedy and don't trust one another. When they do, the Monarchists will rise in revolt. While they fight for control of their land, they will leave us here in the hill country alone. Maybe not for long, but maybe for long enough."

"Long enough for what?"

With a deft gesture she wove a knot of light out of the

air. It illuminated Diyana's expression caught in startled delight at the Lamp's beauty. At its unwavering glow.

"For whatever we make of it. Maybe we can make a deal with the Monarchists."

"A deal?"

"Independence in exchange for alliance. Maybe there is more even than that. Maybe there is another path, a way to live without Liberationists or Monarchists. For us, and maybe also for the servants and laborers and prisoners in their land, if we can persuade them there's a chance for a different life if we join together."

"Bold words. Big words. Dangerous words."

"That's what they told my parents, isn't it? When they arrested them for teaching people to read and write. Words are too dangerous and too bold for the likes of you. But all that means is they want to keep us obedient and ignorant. There's more to magecraft than what they teach at the asylums. There's more to the world than we are allowed to know. Why not, aunt? Why not be bold? Our chance is coming."

Fellian raised the Lamp. Its light spilled over them, chased down the length of the passage whose walls they stood inside, glinting on the brass latches of each unopened door.

ACKNOWLEDGMENTS

My heartfelt thanks to the fabulous and impressive team at Tordotcom Publishing: my most excellent editor, Lee Harris (thanks for asking me!); tireless editorial assistants Sanaa Ali-Virani and Matt Rusin; copy editor Christina MacDonald; proofreaders Sui Mon Wu and Rachel Weinick; production manager Jim Kapp; production editor Megan Kiddoo; designer Heather Saunders; jacket designer Christine Foltzer; ad/promo designer Amy Sefton; the ace marketing team of Becky Yeager, Renata Sweeney, Amanda Melfi, and Michael Dudding; the indefatigable publicists Caroline Perny and Saraciea Fennell; and of course publisher Irene Gallo. Special shout-out to Tommy Arnold for the gorgeous cover illustration.